GULLY & GRACE 2

TOY

CHAPTER 1

ully

This was some bullshit that I was witnessing right now. I didn't come here to see all this soap opera shit. Russ looked at me I know he's thinking the same thing that I'm thinking.

"If your husband is buried somewhere why the fuck you ain't go dig his ass up? Why come got me to buy the land? You could've done that on your own. You don't need me," I told Martina.

"Martina you never told me you had anything to do with Lester's disappearance. What do you mean you buried him?" Her father asked with tears in his eyes.

"You aren't gonna sit here and disrespect me by showing you're hurt about your old lover. I thought you've done away with all that. I told you that you should've never involved Martina in this in the first place. The entire scenario is awkward and disgusting," the mother said.

"Now is not the time for all that. We can talk about this later," the father said attempting to shut the mother down.

"Oh you think we're getting out of this alive? There are men with guns in here. I know you're not that stupid. Well, then again, you lost our family's fortune so you just might be," she continued.

"Yo!!! Can you two shut the fuck up. Martina why didn't you just dig your husband up?" I asked looking at her.

All this back and forth had me ready to kill the whole damn family and take my ass home. I needed answers though before I do that plus I needed to make Blaine's ass suffer.

"It's hard to dig him up when your company's building on it," she said.

"Hold up, you said you wanted to buy some property so you could dig his ass up yourself. Now you're telling me he's under the apartment building I'm working on. Which one is it? I still think you're lying about something else. You just give off that lying ass bitch vibe. He can't be under that building anyway because he would've been found when they dug to put the pipes down. Something's not right about all this shit," I said.

"Huh?" Martina's dumb ass asked me.

She was so stupid that she didn't even think none of this shit through. It was apparent that she was still playing games. Here it is we have guns and are clearly here to do some damage but, she thinks things are still a game. I was fighting off getting pissed but, then I decided that she needed to see that other side of me. Martina was up to something and it was more than that bullshit ass story was about her husband. I lifted my gun and shot her father in the right shoulder. The family jumped in shock and fear at the fact that I did shoot the old man. They were gonna meet the Gully that I hadn't let loose in years.

"Just leave our parents out of this. They have nothing to do with the reason why you're here. You shouldn't have come here in the first place," Blaine said.

I shifted my head to the side so that I was looking at him sideways. He had to have lost his mind talking to me about leaving someone out of this. His ass was the reason I was here. I shot Blaine in both his knees. He dropped to the floor screaming out in pain with tears falling.

"Do y'all see that shit fellas? Bad ass Blaine is now on the floor crying because his punk ass can't take the pain," I said laughing.

I walked over to where he was laying. I know he couldn't get himself together so he was rocking from side to side.

"Leave him alone," Martina said.

I gave her the look of death which made her shut her damn mouth. If she kept fucking around she was going to be the next one to get a bullet. I turned my attention to the booty bandit named Blaine.

"What were you trying to accomplish by putting your hands on Grace? It's not like you want to be with her. You and her haven't been together in a while. Yet, you take your ass over there to beat on her for what reason?" I asked him.

It was comical looking at him trying to concentrate on what I was saying but, the pain he was in wouldn't let him focus completely. I had him right where I wanted him to be. The pain he was in meant that he wasn't in the frame of mind to where he could think up a lie. Pain is the easiest way to get someone to talk. The need for the pain to stop will make them tell on their parents, dog, and neighbors.

"I...I didn't mean for it to go that far. I was only going to talk to her. She wasn't supposed to be pregnant. Finding out that she was pregnant made me lose it. I don't remember hitting her. When I realized what I had done I wanted to die," he said.

"No worries you'll get what you want soon enough."

"He's bleeding everywhere," the mother said.

"Patch his ass up then or shut the fuck up," Russ said.

I know he's irritated with this entire situation. Truthfully, I'm irritated with it as well. I came to fuck Blaine up not find out about a dead body that was supposed to be buried on one of the properties that I'm developing. This shit was getting outrageous.

The mother went to the bathroom bringing back a first aid kit. She slammed it down on the table with an attitude.

"You want me to shoot your wig off. I know your old ass don't think we gives a fuck about your attitude having ass. You needed to have an attitude when you found out your husband was a damn fruit loop. You got life fucked up. I don't want to shoot old ladies but, I will if you keep slamming shit around this motherfucker," Quell said.

I almost forgot his ass was here. Russ started laughing at how mad Quell looked.

"Leave that damn lady alone. You know we don't hurt old women and kids. You're tripping," Russ told him.

"Nah, if I have a flash back of my high school days and think that she's my bitch ass English teacher then I'd be tripping. We don't fuck with the innocent women and kids. If a kid stole my wallet or some shit I'm fucking they ass up. Just like if she keeps testing me I'm gonna shoot her damn wig off. The shit is simple as fuck to understand. Her ass ain't innocent she raised these simple motherfuckers. If you think about it everything going on is her fucking fault. She pushed their scandalous asses out of her twat," Quell said sounding serious as hell.

"Germain you need to find another way to handle the situation. We need to find out what we need to do about the body," Martina said.

"We? I already told your ass about calling me Germain. Keep fucking testing me, Martina. Nah, your ass needs to figure the shit out. See you thought by telling me that the body is on the property that my company's working on was gonna make me help your murdering ass. It's not though. If the body is ever found under the building it's not gonna make them folks come arrest me. Like I said before if he was down there he would've been found," I told her.

"Are you calling me a liar? What reason would I have to lie about any of this?" She asked.

Martina was lying her ass off I just couldn't understand why. She may have wanted me to just come running to help her and believe anything that she was saying. Too bad I'm not built like that. I don't believe anything that she's saying but, that only means I can't kill her tonight. I need to find out what the fuck her deal is before I kill her. I'm sure that time will come soon enough. Martina's not one of these woman that will just live her life and leave me out of her shit. She's gonna try to find any and every way to get me to help her. I'm not helping her though. I was never on that type of time with her before now. We were fucking and that's it. Now she can't get that from me either. She was only gonna get her life taken when everything is said and done.

"Martina, you can leave."

Russ looked at me crazy when I said that. Martina even looked surprised. There was a method to my madness though.

"Are you serious?" She asked.

"Yeah, you can go. Tonight isn't about you it's about Blaine and his need to beat on Grace. I know I don't have to tell you this but, I will anyway. If you tell anybody about what went on in here I'll choke the life out of you with my bare hands."

"What are we going to do about Lester's body?" She asked.

"This motherfucker and the word *we*, what the fuck is wrong with her ass," Quell said.

"You have to handle your own shit," I told her.

She looked disappointed that I wasn't going to help her. In my opinion she could leave his ass where he is. No body equals no case.

"Gully just think about it," she told me.

"You can walk out of here with your life or get carried out with your brother by the coroner. The choice is yours." She turned to walk out of the door. I gave Russ a head nod and he took out his phone to make the call. He slipped his phone back in his pocket. I looked at the mother who was still patching up the father's shoulder. "I need you to call the ambulance for your son fifteen minutes after we leave." I said as I stood up making sure to step on one of the knees that was still bleeding. "You're gonna tell the police that three white guys high on some shit shot your ass. Trust me this conversation isn't over. If you tell them anything other than that you'll die a lot quicker than I plan."

He nodded his head up and down fast as hell. I gave the fellas the head nod and we left out of the house. We were quiet walking to the car. I was thinking hoping that all of this turned out the way I had planned it.

"Do you think she's gonna lead us to anything?" Russ asked.

"All we can do is wait. Let Ralph know that he isn't supposed to take his eyes off her at all. I want him to stick to her ass like glue."

"If this shit falls the way you think it is remind me to never cross your ass. You're a smart motherfucker that's for sure. Just drop me off at the crib I know y'all want to get to the hospital," Quell said.

He was right about that I wanted to lay up under Grace for the rest of the night. I know the next couple of weeks were gonna be hard for all of us. The last thing I wanted to do was have her worry about shit. I was gonna handle everything. All she had to do was get better. Me on the other hand; I'm excited to say let the games begin.

CHAPTER 2

drian

Rolling around on the floor of the elevator with a messed up ankle was not what I wanted to be doing right now. I only wanted to get a snack from the cafeteria. Here I was though adrenaline rushing so much that I wasn't feeling the pain of the ankle or the arm which were both hurt before this bitch decided to approach me. I was on her ass fighting for my damn life. She had the right motherfucker today.

"Stupid bitch how fucking dare you approach me about this shit. Your ass has been done with Russ. I hate all you can't let go bitches. You got life fucked up today," I said as I hit her in her face.

She was trying but, failing to fight me off of her. She couldn't get it together because I wasn't letting up off her. Suddenly I was pulled off her. I was so busy beating her ass that I didn't know the elevator had started or that we had arrived on a floor.

"Ma'am you have to calm down," the fat bologna smelling security guard said as I tried to get away from him to continue beating that bitch's ass.

"I want her arrested! She attacked me for no reason!" She yelled.

"Ma'am you do know we have cameras on every floor and every corner of this building. Are you sure you want to make false statements?" another security guard asked.

"False statement? That bitch attacked me. Look at her then look at me," she said.

"It appears that she got the better of you. We watched on the cameras how you were all up on her in the cafe. We saw how you confronted her, how you hit the stop button in the elevator. We saw it all," he told her.

"Wait a minute having cameras on the elevator is a violation of my privacy," she said.

"No, that's the bathroom that you're thinking off. Cameras on the elevator is a normal thing. You never know what may happen. I need to ask you to turn around and put your hands behind your back."

"You can't arrest me. I just told you that she attacked me. I want my lawyer," she continued.

"I'm sure you do. I need you to turn around though. When the city's police gets here you can tell them that you want a lawyer and a phone call. Can you please turn around? If I have to wrestle you down to the ground it won't turn out good for you," he told her.

"I'm not doing shit. You just said yourself that you're not a real cop. You're just a glorified flashlight with two legs. You can't do shit to me Day-Day," she said.

I shook my head because it was clear he was about to make her turn around. He did just that. I watched as he wrestled her down to the ground. He placed the cuffs on her but, she was still squirming around talking shit. This bitch must be crazy in real life. Once she was cuffed he stood her up on her feet. She was jerking away from him the best way that she could.

"Ma'am do you want to press charges. Either way she'll be going to the police station. She's caused a public disturbance," the white guard told me.

"Yo! What the fuck is going on here?" I heard Russell say from behind us.

I turned around to see him and Gully standing there looking at us. He looked so sexy in his all black that my body started reacting to him. I licked my lips as I thought about the nasty things I wanted him to do to me. He looked at me and smirked because he knew where my head was.

"Sir, do you know these two women?" The fat guard asked.

"This one is my wife," he said pointing at me.

"Wife! Wife! You fucking married her. I hope she's ready to play step mama because I'm pregnant with your baby!" She yelled.

Gully and Russ looked at each other and started laughing loud and hard as hell. Those two needed some mental help. I didn't see anything funny about it. If this bitch was pregnant by Russell I was gonna be fighting his ass when we got home later. I wasn't leaving because I know that Russell and I belonged together there was no question in my mind about that but, my foot was gonna belong up his ass if any of this was true.

"Caretha miss me with that 'I'm pregnant' bullshit. If you think that my ass was so pussy whipped that I would even think about going up in you raw your ass needs to be committed. You must've forgotten who you're dealing with I'm smarter than the average nigga. You thought you were getting over by giving me those condoms with the holes punched in them. Well guess the fuck what. I was playing your ass too. Every time we went out to eat, I went to pick up food for you, or even gave your ass some water from the kitchen you were getting served up a crushed up plan B pill too. How about them mother-fucking apples?" Russell said with a big ass smile.

Caretha looked like he had just gut punched her ass. The color drained from her face and her jaw dropped. It was funny because she thought she had his ass. I could only shake my head at her desperate behavior. She was trying everything and anything she could.

"You're looking real desperate right now. Just take it, you and Russell are done," I said.

"It's not over until I say it is. He's mine bitch!" She screamed.

"Okay, we've had enough of that. The police should be on the way." The guard took her by her arm walking her down the hallway. The fat guard was still standing in front of me.

"Yo! Charlie you can back the fuck up. You're standing too close," Russell said.

"I need a statement from her," he said.

"No you don't just look at the fucking camera and write down what you see. That shit can't be that damn hard."

Russell was standing beside me now looking at the guard. He was doing that man thing where he's daring him to make a move or say something out of the way but, the guard never did. He looked at Gully then to Russell before walking away.

"I need to get back to the room with Grace," I said before walking away from Russell.

"Hold up, I know you're not pissed with me. I ain't know her bitch ass was going to try you," Russell told me.

"Russell just go 'head with all that. You may not have known but, with a track record like hers you should've expected it. She went to my mother's house with a lie before. Why wouldn't she come up here to try to get at me? Why wouldn't she lie and say she's pregnant? Why wouldn't she try to get me arrested? Huh, can you answer that. I never thought you would underestimate the things a desperate woman will go through. So you standing here telling me that you didn't know means nothing to me. Nobody knew but, we both should've been prepared for it," I told him.

I wasn't blaming him for her actions but, he should've known that she wasn't going to just let shit be. It didn't matter how much he threatened her, she wasn't going to let the shit go. She wasn't going to stay quiet. Even now I understood that I had to be prepared for the unexpected. This was going to be the last time somebody caught my ass slipping. After leaving Russell standing in the hallway I made my way back to Grace's room. I saw her and Gully sitting, talking, and smiling. I really prayed that he was the one that could help her find some true happiness.

"You good sis?" Gully asked.

"I'm fine. I just have to condition myself to stay aware of my surroundings at all times. I don't know why I didn't think that it was her when I first saw her. This isn't gonna make me leave Russell though. I'm in this for the long haul. He doesn't have to worry about that. I just have to carry myself different," I told him.

"So you're not pissed with me anymore," Russell asked as he came in the room.

"I was never pissed with you. I'm just disappointed that neither of us thought that she was gonna do some more stupid shit," I told him.

"I get what you're saying but, instead of standing here fake beefing with me we need to be prepared for the next time. If she ever makes it that far, fucking with me I'll go hunt her ass down," he told me.

"No, there's no need for you to go looking for trouble. She's getting booked tonight so that gives us a few days to get everything we need into place."

"She's right and you know it Russ. Get some of the guys to watch out for the women when we're not around. Grace is in the hospital so they'll just need to sit out front to make sure no one that ain't supposed to be here tries to get in. If it's not family or the staff they don't get in period. I don't put anything past anyone. Shit, even though Blaine is more than likely in a wheel chair I still don't doubt that he'll try his hand. As a matter of fact I'm hoping and praying that he does. That way I can kill his ass without consequence. You know it's not about what they think but, what they can prove."

"He filled me in on what went down at the house. At first I didn't understand why he let them live but, I get it now. They'll definitely try their hands again. I know that Blaine told y'all that this was all behind me helping him keep up appearances but, I still think there's something else. He seems real stalker like for someone who needs my help," Grace said.

I know I'm a little on the hyped up side but, I know Russ and Gully didn't just exchange a look. Grace must've seen it too because she looked at me with a crazy look. I hoped she didn't go off on Gully about some shit that she doesn't know all the details about. With everything else going on she doesn't need to start an argument prematurely.

"Yeah, that's why I brought her this baby gun to put under her pillow. She knows how to shoot so she'll be good if something does pop off," Gully said.

"Don't be like me and leave your gun everywhere but where it needs to be. I'm so tired of getting caught out here without it. I promise the next person that approaches me on some bullshit will be getting a bullet in the middle of the forehead," I told them.

We stayed around talking for a few more hours. We met the guy that would be standing outside of Grace's room and the one that will be tailing me. Not too long after that Russell and I headed home. I was tired and I just wanted a hot bath and a bed. I wanted some peace even though I know it's going to be temporary.

CHAPTER 3

uss

I was downstairs punching the punching bag. I was fighting the urge to bail Caretha out of jail just so I can beat her ass with my bare hands. I know if I do that then I was gonna have to fight Adrian too. I'm not a man that will beat on a chic but, Caretha was surely gonna be the first female that I torture the shit out of. I couldn't just sit around waiting on her to come at Adrian again. I was thinking of all the shit that I could do while torturing her ass when Adrian came down interrupting my thoughts. I looked at her and noticed that she was dressed in all black. My first thought was if she had on a black panties and bra set to complete her look. I licked my lips causing her to laugh at me.

"What's up? You 'bout to go on a caper or something?" I asked.

"Can you hear me out first?" She responded.

I instantly stopped hitting the bag. I knew she was about to come at me with some crazy shit.

"I'm listening."

"We need to bail ole' girl out. That way when we get her out we can fuck her up instead of waiting for her to come for me. I know she's not expecting us to bail her ass out. We have the element of surprise on our side," she said.

"You're not thinking this all the way through. If we bail her out that's going to leave our names on the paper work. When she doesn't show for court we're the first ones that will be questioned about her whereabouts."

She stood there thinking about what I just said for a few minutes. A smile slowly spread across her face. I got a little anxious and turned on at her expression.

"Get one of your workers to do it. If they do it then they won't be able to connect us to her. Either way we have to get her ass out before someone else does. Baby you know I'm right," she said.

"Go take your kick in the door outfit off. Get you some sleep tonight. Let me make a few phone calls. I'll have everything lined up for tomorrow. Don't get up in the morning asking me all kinds of questions about the plan either."

She stomped off like she was a little girl that I told she couldn't have any ice cream. It's a damn shame that sweet innocent Adrian was long gone. My woman was ready to ride beside her man that was some sexy shit right there. I was about to start back punching the bag when I thought about her in the room taking her clothes off. I took the gloves off tossing them onto the floor. I made my way to the bedroom and there she was bent over sliding down the sweatpants that clung to her body. I took my shorts off before walking over to her, sliding her panties, which were indeed black, to the side and sliding myself inside of her folds. She moaned and tried to get away from me but, I had my hands gripping her waist. She wasn't going to get away from me, not right now. I pumped in and out of her with the urgency of a man that had something to prove. I didn't have to prove shit but, I wanted her to understand the hunger and desire I had for her right now. There was no other place I would want to be. Thinking about her holding a gun to the head of Caretha and pulling the trigger sent me over the edge. She screamed out as she came with me. We both fell onto the bed breathing hard and relaxed.

"Damn, what was that all about?" She asked.

"I just had to have you Adrian. Seeing you all in gangsta bitch mode is sexy as fuck and if you keep it up you're gonna end up pregnant. I know it was quick but, that was just a taste. Go 'head get in the shower and don't put a stitch of clothes on. After I make some phone calls I'm gonna dive in for the rest of the night," I told her.

She laughed at me like I was playing. I was dead ass serious right now. The way she had me feeling I wouldn't be surprised if I end up fucking her on the way to the warehouse. Shit, she could at least suck me off in the parking lot before we go inside.

"Something is wrong with you. I can't believe that doing what needs to be done is what turned you on that much."

"Where did this new Adrian come from? You were never like this when you were younger. Now you're all in with going to fuck ole' girl up. What's with the change? I'm not complaining, just wondering what the deal is."

"After I got settled into my new environment I started taking self defense classes. I didn't have anyone else to fall back on so I had to take care of me. I took time to learn how to shoot. Obtained my gun license and all that. I think it was a year that I had been gone. The holidays had rolled around. I wanted to come home but, at the same time I didn't want to. I ended up staying there. I walked to the corner store and on the way back I was robbed at gun point. I could tell they were just as scared as I was. They were young as hell. I would say they were no more than fourteen years old. I fought them off somewhere during the tussle I was shot in the shoulder. I didn't tell anyone because I didn't want to ruin anyone's holiday. No one was with me in town so all I had to do was not mention it when I was on the phone with them. The feeling of fighting them off was exhilarating. I was proud that I didn't just let whatever happen go down without fighting back. I've been fighting back ever since," she told me.

"Damn you've been to hell and back I see. Do you realize that although you get upset with yourself about not having the gun when you need it; you still end up protecting yourself and those around you without it. I admire you for your strength and determination. You are unbelievable and you don't even know it. While you're walking around pissed at yourself I'm standing next to you with a hard dick because you being so strong is so fucking sexy."

I gave her a kiss after expressing to her how I feel. This woman was all that and five bags of chips in my eyes. It could be that the love I have for her was clouding my perception but, it was what it was. She was my black pantherette and no one could change my view of her. Just hearing that she had been robbed or almost robbed but, she got herself out of it by protecting herself was admirable. She was everything to me in my eyes.

"I'm just wondering if you're this worked up behind me talking about it; I wonder what will happen when you see me in action. I may just come out of all this knocked up," she said with a smile.

"I wouldn't mind you walking your sexy ass around here with a growing belly. That shit will be sexy as hell," I told her as I gripped my hardening dick.

"Let me find out that you were out here getting hard for all your little hoes like you are for me right now," she said giving me the side eye.

"Oh hell nah, none of that was going on. Most of the time I had to already be horny when I hooked up with them to get the nut off. You have a different effect on me. You can smile at me and my dick gets hard. Sometimes when you say my name the tone of your voice makes my dick hard. That day I saw you in the hospital and I was waiting for you to come to the parking garage my dick was hard just thinking about touching you again. You make my body feel things that only you being near me causes. No one has ever given me the feelings that you give me. I love you baby. You complete me."

She gave me a kiss then got up to take her shower. I hope she understood that I was talking from my heart. She was all that I ever needed from a woman. If she goes through with what she plans to do to Caretha I just might marry her ass right there in front of Caretha's dead body. Just thinking about it made me want to go dick her down in the shower. I had calls to make but, they can wait for a few minutes.

OOOOO

I stood in the doorway looking at her sleep. I held the small blue velvet box in my hands. After making the calls that needed to be made last night I couldn't find sleep for shit. Thats when I got up to get the ring that had been tucked away in the back of the safe. The ring that I was supposed to give her before she dipped on me. The ring that was only going to be on her finger. I still had a hard time believing that she was here with me. This is where she belonged, in my bed naked as the day she was born. The day that she was born for me. I was having second thoughts of giving it to her so soon. There was too much going on right now but, this was something that couldn't wait. We had wasted all those years apart from one another. Right now there was no way I was gonna let her go another day with doubts in her head. I wasn't crazy I know that she was having her doubts but, what woman wouldn't knowing that I had ran through women like they were six packs of beers. It wasn't a secret that I was out there in the worst way when it came to women. That was only because she was the one for me. When I lost her I lost a piece of myself it wasn't because of the baby either. It was because of *her* the woman that made me want to be a better man. My phone alerting me that I had a text coming in brought me out of my daydream of dicking Adrian down after she became my wife. It was cool what we did last night but, I owed her more than sex as my woman or girlfriend. She was so much more than that. Once all this was over she was going to be my wife. I put that on everything. Looking down at the phone as I slid the box into my pocket.

Ms. Wet-Wet: I haven't heard from you. Can you come thru today. I need it.

Me: Nah I can't do that. You need to be calling someone else to scratch that itch from her on out

Ms. Wet-Wet: Y?

Me: I can't fuck with you like that no more.

Ms. Wet-Wet: What did I do for you to cut me off?

Me: Nothing…. You're just not her

Ms. Wet-Wet: Are you trying to tell me you got a woman or something? I thought you weren't looking for a relationship.

Me: Just don't hit me up no more.

Ms. Wet-Wet: You still haven't said why the change up? Just tell me what I did? I thought we were working towards something.

Me: Nah, I was just working towards a nut with you. All that is done now.

Ms. Wet-Wet: Can you just tell me why?

Me: I told you. You're not her. Call up one of those other niggas. Shit, you can call your homegirl if you want. JUST STOP CALLING ME

Ms. Wet-Wet: whoever she is she's not gonna want you when I talk to her.

Me: Oh yeah. Go 'head tell her whatever you want shawty. I hope you know how to stick and move though. I promise you shit is gonna go left.

Ms. Wet-Wet: we'll see

Me: I tried to warn yo ass but, aye do what you feel. You playing yourself by begging me for some dick. When you see me don't speak. It was nice while it lasted tho.

These chic's swore they were good with the just fucking arrangement that I had with them. If she was cool with us just fucking then why was her retarded ass begging after I told her we were done. Bitches swore they had the pussy that could change a nigga's mind. They didn't understand that pussy was just pussy. It wasn't my problem though.

"I hope you're telling that bitch that you're not fucking with her no more. Don't make me nut up and have to kick ass behind you. You know I will," Adrian said to me.

I didn't even notice that her ass was sitting up in the bed looking at me text this bitch. That's why Adrian was gonna be my wife. She had no problem calling me out on my shit.

"That's exactly what I told her. Come on so I can cook you some breakfast. I have a surprise for you after we eat. Make sure you dress in all black."

She smiled at me making me laugh at her.

"Good I need to blow off some steam today," she said.

I watched her naked ass walk into the bathroom. I wanted to

follow her but, we had shit to do. I could fuck her all night long after we handle the problem at hand. I shook my head at her because she was gonna end up pregnant sooner than later. She knows that gangsta shit made my dick hard.

race

I woke up to Gully texting on his phone. He was dressed in some gray sweat pants, white t-shirt and some gray and white Adidas on his feet. I thought he was sexy in the suits that I had grown accustomed to seeing him in. Seeing him dressed down let me know that he could be sexy in anything that he wore. He was just a sexy ass man period.

"Are you just gonna be a damn creep looking at me and not saying nothing?" he asked not even looking away from his phone.

"What really happened last night? I still feel like something is missing from all of this. You should've taken his ass out. I understand why you didn't but, I still want him dead. I hope he doesn't come back to hurt me again. I never thought he would do what he did in the first place. Do you think he'll do that?" I asked.

"Calm down killa. He's still alive but, he's somewhat incapacitated I doubt if he even speaks to you if you see him in public."

"Do you think you'll be able to find out whatever it is that you're looking for?"

"Oh I am sure that I'll get the answers before I take him and his sister out."

"What sister? You never said anything about a sister last night," I told him. I knew when him and Russ exchanged looks that something was being left out.

"Blaine's sister is one of my former freaks named Martina. I could've killed the whole family last night but, I need to be sure that when I do kill them there won't be anything that I don't know about that'll come back on us in the future. How do you feel?"

I had more questions but, I'll leave it alone for now. If he didn't kill Blaine I know there had to be a reason. I didn't have the energy to argue with him about it right now.

"I'm sore but I'll be fine. When am I getting out of here? I have a life and a lounge to run."

"You're not going to work for the rest of the month you need the mental and physical rest. You just lost our baby, Grace."

"Do you think I needed you to remind me of that? I know what the hell I lost. I know you didn't forget that I was the one carrying the baby inside me Gully," I told him with and attitude.

"I'm not saying it because I think you forgot. When did you start calling me Gully? Don't make me show you why they call me Gully. You've been calling me Germain, don't switch that shit up now. You don't even sound right calling me Gully. Don't make me fuck you up. If you have some shit to say then say the shit. You throwing me attitude ain't gonna make me leave this room or help you get to work any quicker."

We engaged in a staring war. If he thought he was gonna keep me from going to work he was gonna have a fight on his hands. I needed to get back into my normal routine to help me stay sane. I would've thought he understood that shit about me.

"I need to go back to work to keep my mind off of what happened," I revealed to him.

"I know you don't think avoiding it is gonna help you. I can tell you that avoiding the shit is only gonna make it worse. I get that you want to go back to work but, that ain't happening Grace. You can sit there with that fucked up attitude all you want. That attitude doesn't move me. I'm only looking out for you," he told me.

Just when I was going to tell his ass how I felt about him and all his damn demands. Auntie GiGi and Rick walked in.

"Y'all good?" Rick asked looking between the two of us.

"Nah, she's hard headed as fuck. Her ass is pissed that I told her she needs to take some time off before going back to work," Germain volunteered.

"He's right Grace. You need some time to deal with what happened," Auntie GiGi said.

Of course, she was going to agree with him. She was my aunt but she was definitely team Gully all the way. He could do no wrong in her eyes and she just met his ass. I rolled my eyes because I didn't give a shit what either of them said. I was going back to work and there ain't shit that either of them could do about it. I could show them both better than I could tell them. I wasn't pregnant anymore so Germain had no say so in what I did or didn't do. He had me fucked up.

"I'm fine. The sooner I can go back to being productive like I was before all of this the better."

Germain shook his head at my words. Rick was laughing like a damn idiot while Auntie GiGi was just looking at my ass. Auntie popped Rick on the back of his head.

"What you hitting me for?"

"Because, there ain't a damn thing funny that's why, Richard don't make me do it again. You're always laughing at the wrong shit. If that was one of your little hoes that went through what Grace went through you would understand that. Some times I wonder about your ass. Losing a child can be the most detrimental thing to happen to a woman. Especially when it comes at the hand of a jealous motherfucker. Trust me I know what she's going through all too well." I looked at Auntie GiGi wondering what the hell she was talking about. "Can y'all step out for a minute so I can talk to Grace?" She asked.

Germain and Rick left without saying a word.

"What's going on?" I asked her.

"I know you don't remember but, I was pregnant once. I had the nerve to be pregnant with twins at that. I wasn't high risk like you though. I was happy as hell to have the chance to bring two knuckle head children into the world. All that changed though. The man that I was knocked up by was a guy that I called myself being in love with. He was the best thing created since sliced bread in my eyes. My brothers didn't like him though. I had to pull Geon off his ass a time or two. They all tried to warn me that he was bad news but, I was too in love to listen to anything that anybody had to say," She paused shaking her head. I could see the pain in her eyes.

"You don't have to talk about it if it's too painful," I told her.

"No, you need to understand that Gully is only looking out for you. I know you don't want to listen to what he has to say because you don't want to feel like you're giving him control over you. Just listen to me," she said.

"Okay, I'll listen," I told her.

"One night I was over at your dad's house for one of those parties that he used to have with all the old people from the neighborhood we grew up in. You know your father was a big deal but, he never moved like one. He stayed in contact with the people we grew up with. If he wasn't at work, in court, or working on a case he always acted the same as he always had. Anyway, I was at the house with everybody. We were having a good time playing cards, drinking, and talking shit. Although I was pregnant at the time your dad was sure to slide me a glass or two of red wine. I got home around two in the morning from the party that night. When I got home all the lights were out. It was quiet as a church full of hookers. I could feel that something wasn't right. As soon as I walked into the bedroom I was punched in the face.

He started talking about how I was sitting around my brother's house talking shit about him. He even accused me of sleeping with a few of the guys at the house that night. I tried to fight him back with all I had but, he ended up beating me so bad that I lost my kids that night."

Auntie GiGi was crying now. She kept her composure but, the tears still fell.

"Oh my goodness Auntie I had no idea."

"I know you didn't. You were young as hell then. You wouldn't know because none of us ever talked about it. After losing my kids I promised myself that I would never let another man get away with putting his hands on me or you. You became my child that night. I didn't want to go through the pain of losing another baby at the hands of him," she said.

"What happened to the guy?" I asked.

"I called my brothers from the hospital. Once I told them what happened they asked me if I was done with him. I told them that I was done, they said they would take care of it. When I was released from the hospital they had moved me into a new house. I never asked what they did to him and they never told me."

"Auntie GiGi what does that have to do with my situation?" I asked.

"I told you all that so you could understand that Gully isn't like that. He isn't telling you not to go to work because he wants to control you. He's only telling you that because he cares. You may be fine right now but, what about when you go home and you start having dreams about that night. You may feel like you're fine but, trust me this is just the beginning. The time will come when you're at home in the shower and you find yourself crying uncontrollably because you feel that pain and sense of loss. Then there will be times that you blame yourself for not doing something although none of this is your fault. The guilt, tears, shame, hurt, and regret will still come. Let him be there for you. I can promise you that you don't want to go through this alone. I know you're strong. Allowing him to be there isn't gonna make you weak. It makes you smart," she told me.

I was quiet for few minutes allowing her words to sink in. The words shock and unexpected came to mind. I guess that's what my uncle was talking about the night of my grand opening. I didn't remember any of what she said going on. I didn't even remember her having a boyfriend. I could see why she hasn't allowed any men into her life after that. My heart ached for her. I wonder if when she looks at her nieces and nephews does she think of the twins that she never had. I already had the utmost respect for her but, after hearing that story I know for damn sure she's my superwoman. I never saw her cry besides when someone in the family died or was hurt. She never appeared to be broken in any way. Now that I knew for sure she has been scared and damaged that made me have hope for myself. Maybe I should stop being difficult with Germain and allow him to love and protect me like the boss that he is.

CHAPTER 5

ully

I wasn't paying that I'm going to work shit no mind while Grace was talking. She just didn't know I had already changed the locks on her office door. The security, bartenders, and manager of the lounge were all informed to call me if she walks her ass in here before she had time to relax and mentally recuperate from what happened. I wasn't a psychiatrist or nothing but, I know that she needed to sit her ass down somewhere. I don't know what her and Auntie GiGi were talking about but, I hope she got through to her because I would hate to have to tie her up for her to chill out.

"Aye, don't be over there thinking nasty thoughts about my cousin while I'm standing right next to you. That shit is disrespectful," Rick said.

"I wasn't thinking nothing nasty. I just want her to be okay. After some shit like that it can change a person. It affects you like when you catch your first body. She'll never be the same. I know she thinks that she can just jump up and do whatever.

She can't do that. I mean she could physically but, her mental is gonna be all fucked up if she keeps avoiding it. Holding shit in leads to breakdowns and shit," I told him.

"Yeah, I feel it. You know she's not all there. She always wants to be in control so I know her dealing with this shit is killing her inside. She couldn't control what dude did and her going back to work is just a way for her to feel like she's in control of something."

I understood where he was coming from but, that shit wasn't happening on my watch. I don't care if I have to sit down in the middle of the floor with her and hold her while she cries. I'm gonna be here for her even if she doesn't want me to.

"Yeah, well she's gonna have to take a back seat for a while. I got her though there's no doubt about that."

Auntie GiGi stuck her head out of the door and waved us back into the room. When I walked back in the room I felt a shift in the air.

"Why everybody looking all crazy? What happened in here? Auntie GiGi are you pregnant?" Rick asked trying to break the ice in the air.

"If I was pregnant don't be asking about it if you not gonna help take care of it," Auntie GiGi answered.

"You better not be out here acting like some young thot. That shit ain't cute to be an old hoe," Rick said.

"Well, I guess you better call your hoe ass daddy and tell him that. Everybody knows he was out here fucking with them young chics that's what made his old ass have a heart attack. If you wanna start giving advice on what people need to do with their private parts then start with him and his old ass ding-a-ling."

"Can you two not go at it today? I can't be adding days to my stay here because I've re-injured myself laughing at y'all," Grace said.

"Tell pussy monitor that. I don't give a damn what he does with them Instagram thots that he deal with. He need to get off me and my business," Auntie GiGi said.

"You should act your age," Rick told her.

"You should act your dick size. You got me fucked up. You're just my damn nephew you don't get any special privileges for that."

"I'm glad you ain't my mama because if you were we would have problems," Rick said.

"Do you even know your mama?"

Now we were all laughing so hard that tears were coming out of our eyes. Auntie GiGi knew she could talk shit with the best of them. She always kept shit real though. You definitely had to have tough skin when you're talking to her.

"Hello, everyone. I can see that the family is all here," the doctor said when he walked in.

He kept looking over at Auntie GiGi. It seemed like he was trying to keep shit professional but, he couldn't stop looking at her. Grace and I exchanged a look letting each other know we saw that bullshit. I was almost afraid to ask what the hell was going on with them.

"Hey doctor, please tell me you're gonna set me free early," Grace said sounding pitiful.

"Actually we are giving you your walking papers. Now before you get excited you're on strict rules not to go back to work for at least three weeks. You will be coming to see me at my office in two days. No strenuous activity, heavy lifting, or excessive walking until then as well."

Grace looked happy as hell that she was getting out of here. I was happy too now I could sleep in my own damn bed. Fucking with these hospital chairs I was gonna have to go to the chiropractor to get my back right. These chairs were murder for a nigga like me. We continued to listen to the instructions that the doctor gave Grace. He walked out after telling everyone goodbye. Ten minutes after he walked out Auntie GiGi left out saying she had to make a call. Grace and I looked at each other and started laughing.

"What was that about?" I asked Grace.

"I have no idea. I know she was saying that she had a date with a man or something the other day. I guess the doctor is the mystery man," she said smiling.

"You know you're coming to the house with me right. I got the gate code changed. There's also two security guards at the gate at all times. I'm not gonna let anything else happen to you or put you in a position that will have you vulnerable again," I told her.

"Okay," she said.

I sat up in my chair looking at her. Ricky was falling out laughing. I know that my face was looking crazy at her right now. I was ready for her to fight with me on the subject. The last thing I was expecting was for her to say okay like she did.

"I think we need to get the nurse in here to check your temperature. You gotta be sick or something to just agree with me like that," I told her.

"I need to talk to you about that," she said then she turned to look at Rick. He kissed his teeth but got up and left the room. Once he left the room she began to talk. "I want to apologize for fighting you on all your decisions regarding me. I understand that you're trying to protect me. It's just that I've gotten used to having to protect myself. I also want to say thank you for not leaving my side. Just keep being patient with me I'm a work in progress."

"No worries I get it. Just know that you're gonna have to do more than challenge my ass on shit for me to walk away from you. Even though the baby didn't make it you're still my baby mama. I would never say or do anything to hurt you. " I told her.

"I understand that. I'm just nervous about what the future holds for us once I get better."

"What do you mean?"

"I'm saying once I'm able to go back to my place then you'll be free to date and fuck like you were before," she told me.

"Hold up, you think because you lost the baby you're gonna lose me?" I asked.

"Yeah, there's nothing to tie us to each other now that I've lost the baby."

"First and foremost you didn't *lose* a damn thing. The baby was taken from the both of us by a little gay ass bitch boy. I don't want you to ever blame yourself for this. All the blame is on his bitch ass," I told her.

"You don't blame me at all? I keep thinking that maybe if I would've talked to him about everything then maybe he wouldn't have reacted the way he did at the house."

"Like I said this ain't your weight to carry. He knew he had bogus intentions when he snuck in the gate. If he was just there to talk or whatever why not announce yourself. He may not have planned it but, he wasn't there on some kumbaya mission. I just need you to talk to me whenever anything is bothering you while you're at the house with me. We're gonna have to talk to each other about any and everything to get past this. I can't have you cracking up on me and having nervous breakdowns and shit."

"I can do that but, don't start complaining when I talk to you so much that your ears start bleeding. I talked with Auntie GiGi and she helped me look at things from a new perspective. I just don't want to get hurt after I open myself up to you," she told me.

She just didn't understand that she was all I wanted. Seeing her go through so much in this little bit of time that we've know each other had caused my feelings to grow deeply for her. The way I saw it I had three to four weeks to show her that I loved her and that she's the one for me.

CHAPTER 6

$\mathcal{A}$untie GiGi

I had to get out of that room. I know Grace noticed how I was looking at Hector. Yes, Hector was the main that I've been secretly dating. Hector and I met at a gas station of all places. He was in line behind me listening to my phone conversation that I was having with one of my good girl friends. I was telling her that I needed too do some squats to firm up my ass so I could catch me a man. I didn't even know he was listening until I went to pump my gas. He came up behind me saying that he would pump the gas for me. I allowed him to pump the gas then he said something to me that should've let me know that he was gonna change my slightly old coochie's life.

"I know as a beautiful black queen you have to handle a lot of things. I just want you to know that a queen should never pump her own gas. There's more that she should be doing with her hands," he told me as he took the gas pump from me.

My mind ain't right as it is so I instantly went to wondering if he had a handful of dick or if I had to hold it with my thumb and forefinger like I was down to the last of a blunt. He caught me licking my lips as I was looking at him. When he was done pumping the gas he stood so close to me I could feel his dick on my thigh. I know he knew what he was doing because he started smiling.

"No need to be scared but, I need to let you know I'm only half aroused," he said then he kissed my neck.

"Do you go around kissing all the women you pump gas for? Are you a pimp or something looking for some vintage hoes to put on the stroll?" I asked serious as hell. He laughed at me like I was joking.

"No, I'm not a Pimp. I'm actually a doctor in regards to my profession as well as other things. Do you always talk to guys you think are pimps? Do you want to be treated like a vintage pussy hoe?" He asked as his eyes raped my body.

I wasn't expecting him to come back at me like he did. He almost knocked me completely off my square.

"You wouldn't know what to do with this vintage grade a pussy young man," I told him.

"Picture that," he said laughing as he came closer to me. "Ain't shit young about this grown man dick that I'm wanting to put so far inside you that you'll feel it in your throat. It's not nice to get a man all hard and shit just to make him go home and choke his dick with his hand causing him to come all over his hand alone."

"How do you know I won't follow your ass home and ride that grown man dick so good that you see the white light to heaven," I responded.

"Is it wet?"

"Yes."

"Is it shaved bald?"

"Yes."

"Is it thumping?"

"Yes."

"What does she taste like?"

"Huh?"

"Don't tell me your not the freak that your body is screaming to me that you are. Did I misjudge you? Did I confuse the hardness of your nipples and the shallowness of your breaths as signs of a woman that doesn't hold back in the bedroom?"

"No you didn't."

"So tell me. What. Does. She. Taste. Like? Did you eat some fruit today and drink your water?"

I was trying to answer him but, the only thing that came out was some gibberish that I didn't even understand.

"You're standing to close," I told him.

"I'm not standing close enough. I would much rather bend you over and be digging in that pussy of yours but, you're out here playing like we aren't grown as fuck. I know I can fuck twelve years of frustration out of you in one night."

"You shouldn't talk about things that you never intend on doing," I told him as I tried to step away from him. He took my hand and forced my body close to his again.

"Oh you're doubting me. Follow me to my house. I can show you a whole lot better than I can tell you. Are you going to follow me or not?" He asked putting my ass on the spot.

"Right now?"

"What's the problem? Do you need to get a babysitter or call your nigga and let him know you gonna go let off some steam for the rest of the night? That is if you have one. I couldn't figure it out from what I over heard in your conversation. Do you have a man?" He asked.

"I don't have kids or a man," I answered.

"Oh well that's even better. So you're stalling because your scared then?" he asked.

"I haven't met a nigga that's scared me in all these years."

"Says the woman with a soaking wet pussy. Just follow me to my place and let me handle that for you. I promise I'll be nice to it. I'll caress it, kiss it, suck it, and fill it up. You gonna follow me or not?"

"Yeah I'm coming," I heard myself say.

I don't know what the hell had gotten into me. I have never acted like this before with a stranger. He licked his lips again looking at me like he was picturing me naked. He turned and walked to his car. I hopped in mine and followed this stranger that I was intending on fucking like some young hoe out here. Regardless of the back and forth that was going on in my head I kept following him.

He pulled into the circular drive way of a house that had to have at least ten rooms in it. I didn't come from a poor family but, this house was all of that. I was so caught up looking at the house that I jumped when he opened the door for me. He took my hand guiding me out of the car. Once I was completely out he closed the door then trapped me between him and the car.

"Can you do me a favor beautiful?"

"Sure," I said too damn enthusiastically.

"I want you to caress that soaking wet treasure of yours a few times, then suck your fingers clean," he said shocking me.

"Now?"

He nodded his head up and down. I asked the lord to forgive me for the acts of depravity, lust, fornication, and any other I was going to commit with this sexy stranger tonight. I also prayed that he was clean because this one night was going to go down condom or no condom. I unbuckled the jeans that I had on. He watched me intently as I slid my hand into my soaked panties.

"That motherfucker is that wet huh?" He asked. He must've noticed my facial expression change. I stood there playing with my pussy while he watched me. "Take your hand out and suck your fingers one by one," he told me. I did exactly as he told me. I showed him that two of my fingers were coated very well. He licked his lips as I licked my fingers. He leaned into me so I could feel his dick jump in his pants. "Hector is the name *that you'll be screaming out tonight as I wear that vintage pussy out. Is there anything that I can't do to this gorgeous body of yours?" I shook my head from side to side.*

"No."

"I expect that's the last time tonight I will hear that word. Come on in here with me so I can rearrange that pussy and change your life," he told me as he lead me into the house.

That night he did things to my body that made me question if I had really been living life. It had to be a crime the way he did my body. I had been going back for more of the same treatment ever since. It was wild how he was in-tune with my body. He knew where the aches were that needed to be touched. He knew where the desire was that needed to be caressed. He was all that and then some. It was a damn shame.

"Georgette," I heard Hector call from behind me.

"Hector, I didn't know you were working on my niece. The night she came here there was another doctor that came out to give us her status," I told him.

"Follow me to my office. We can go into detail there without any distractions."

I did as he instructed me to. I was trying to get out of this place without him seeing me. I needed to create some distance between us before all my clothes fell off. It was crazy how I always ended up naked with a stretched out pussy around him. Just hearing him call my name just now had my panties on their way to being ruined. I had stopped wearing panties when I knew that I was going to see him. Today caught me by surprise so yeah these panties that I had on were gonna be soaked. I walked into the office that he held the door open for me to enter.

"What do we have to discuss Hector that couldn't wait until I came to your house?" I asked.

"Nothing really, I've been having this constant daydream, night dream, fantasy, goal, or ambition to fuck and suck you on my desk. It was just never feasible or should I say the situation never came into play. Seeing you today here was a calling from god to let me know that my dream was about to come true," he told me as he took off his white doctor's coat.

"Hector I think that we're a little too loud for all that to be going on in here."

"This office is sound proof. Take your clothes off Georgette, slowly."

I began to take my clothes off while he took his dick out and massaged it as he looked at me get naked. Once all my clothes were off he started to walk towards me. He took my hand leading me to the desk. I sat on the desk with my bare ass.

"Hector," I said but, he stopped all the words after by collapsing his mouth around my nipple. "Oh shit." I said as I let my head fall back.

He continued to kiss and suck my nipple. Then out of nowhere he forced his bare dick into my opening. There I was in the hospital that I had visited many times in the past but now after this shit here I was gonna walk these halls with an extra pep in my step. Hector just didn't know that not only did his fantasy come true today but, mine did also.

ully

I was sitting in my Camaro waiting on Ralph to get here. Ralph was the person I had watching Martina. He was the perfect person because he was one of those fellas that took *Call Of Duty* to damn far. He didn't just play the game he researched shit. He even went to the lengths of ordering surveillance and security equipment that he had come across on the game. He took this shit more serious than motherfuckers that were enlisted in the military. He did all this but, was a street nigga for sure. It worked to my advantage when situations like this came about. He tapped on the passenger side window letting me know to unlock the doors for him.

"What it do folks?" I asked.

"Are you sure her husband is dead?" He said getting to the point.

"Why you say that?"

I wasn't sure if Lester was dead or not. It just seems off that this man who was known in the community hadn't been reported missing even though Martina lied when she said she tried to. I called down to the station asking questions of my own.

"Just think about it. You're young good looking and you have all this access to the old nigga's money. If he's dead then why the fuck she ain't out here balling out. She hasn't even been out to lunch or dinner. Her online activity hasn't changed either. You said she never wanted to be married in the first place right? If she didn't want to be why is she still acting like she's married. She's not even selling sexual wolf tickets in niggas DMs. Her family hasn't been to see her either."

"Yeah, that's not a surprise to me they have their own shit to worry about. They are the fucked up versions of the Huxtables for sure. I just want to find out what the hell she's doing all this lying for. It has to be a reason and why the fuck is she involving me in the bullshit."

"How's wifey doing?"

"She's good. She's pissed because I'm there to ask her how she feels and all that shit all day long," I said with a chuckle.

"I wish I still had my girl to annoy and shit," he said shaking his head.

His girlfriend used to be into that gaming shit with him but, she changed somewhere down the line. She eventually got tired of trying to get him to change and she dipped on his ass. His way of coping was to get deeper into the gaming shit. Now he was hosting conventions and shit. He was making some money doing the shit too. I was never into sitting in the house all day playing a damn game. It just didn't make sense to me. Ralph changed up my perspective on the shit but, not enough for it to take over my life. I had shit to do and moves to make.

"You'll find one for you soon enough," I told him.

"I'm gonna keep my eye on this bitch for you. If you wanna know what I think, I'll tell you," he said looking at me.

"I'm waiting man what the fuck you stop talking for."

"I think her dad and old boy are trying to run the okie doke on all of them."

"Why you say that?"

"Think about it. What nigga in they right mind gets their daughter to marry the person they love? That shit right there shows you none of them have common sense. Now I understand how he can blow the family fortune. Getting Lester to marry his daughter couldn't have been the only option. He could've left his wife or anything else. Shit, they could've killed the wife's ass. Let me keep watching and digging. They'll fuck up sooner or later," Ralph told me.

We dapped each other up and he went on about his way. I had to stop by *The Cheesecake Factory* to get Grace some pineapple cheesecake before I went to the house. She hasn't been down but, she hasn't been up either. I knew that this would at least put a smile on her face. I just wanted her to try to talk about the loss of the baby at least. She didn't talk much and she damn sure didn't want to talk about it. I just wanted Grace back the one that I was surely falling in love with.

Pulling into the garage I grabbed the bag from *The Cheesecake Factory* and said a silent prayer that things would go well for us tonight. I just wanted to see her happy and smiling. When I got into the house it was dark which meant that she was up in the room watching TV. She was right were I left her a few hours earlier. The TV was on but, I could tell that she wasn't paying it any mind. When I got closer to her there were tears coating her cheeks. Seeing the tears both gave me a sense of relief and concern. I was relieved because she was showing some emotion. The concern came because I never wanted to see her cry.

"He took our baby from us," she said barely above a whisper.

I sat on the bed after slipping my pants and shirt off. I let her lay her head on my chest. I wanted to say so much but everything I thought of saying wasn't going to help the tears stop falling. It wasn't going to make the pain go away that much I know because I'm feeling the same pain that she was right now.

"Let it all out babygirl."

"I know that we made that one in a not-so-fashionable way but, I was getting use to the thought of being someone's mother," she sniffled.

"I get it. I was liking the fact of having a mini me walking around to put his mack game down on all the little girls at daycare and shit."

"Oh no my baby was not gonna be out here running game that early in life."

"Oh but you ain't say he wasn't just that he wasn't that early. I'm cool with that but, by the fifth grade he was gonna have all the hoes," I said laughing.

"I even had thoughts of us being a family one day. How crazy is that?" She said with a little giggle.

"Is it crazy that I still want that with you?" I asked she sat up looking at me.

"Germain, you don't have to want that because I was the one that lost your baby. You don't owe me anything," she said.

"Owe you anything, how can you say that I don't owe you? No, I'm not saying that I want us to be a family because I owe you. I do want us to be a family but only because I know that I love you. I know that one day I'll wake up and be madly in love with you. You put your life on the line to have the baby in the first place. There are a ton of women that would've heard the restrictions that she had on her to bring the baby here safe and they would've checked out of the hospital heading straight to the abortion clinic. You didn't do any of that. You listened and you said you were gonna do all that you could to bring our baby here. If bitch boy wouldn't have done what he did you would be right here pregnant, and pissed with me for making sure you're not doing too damn much. Don't you understand that I didn't have to bring you here with me? I could've gotten a nurse to stay with you twenty-four seven. I could've just FaceTimed your ass a few times a day and went on about my life. I wanted to do all those things for you. I figured if you were gonna do all that to bring me my son then I would make some sacrifices of my own. I wanted to be here when you had one of those stupid ass cravings. All that shit had me excited to be able to experience it with you. Shit if I could knock your ass up again I damn sure would without a second thought. Truthfully I did the first time on purpose," I told her.

She sat up looking at me crazy. This was the first time I had admitted that fact out loud. I surprised myself in telling her of all people. Russ didn't even know about what I did. I mean the sex was bomb as fuck but I was fully aware of what I was doing when I released inside her. I actually said a little prayer for my sperm to find an egg to fertilize.

"Wait a minute. How did you know that I wouldn't get rid of the baby? How did you know if I was gonna tell you about me being pregnant in the first place? You didn't even know if I had a man or anything at the time. You could've fucked up a happy home," she told me.

"I didn't know if you were going to keep it or even tell me to be honest. As for you having a man it was obvious that you didn't. There was no regret in your eyes when I laid your fine ass on the bar. When I was up inside you it didn't feel like no other nigga that mattered had been there. When I slid inside you I knew all of that was all me. Nobody and nothing else mattered," I told her.

"Grace you forgot that you mentioned that you were single. Even Rick said that you were always doing too much when it come to relationships."

She shook her head at me then rolled over onto her side. I could hear her mumbling instead of continuing this conversation. I knew it wasn't over and I'm fine with that. I hope she knows that the next time I get inside her I'm shooting up the club again.

artina

"Daddy this is never gonna work now. I can't believe he didn't kill us all the other night. Have you talked to Blaine? I've been trying to call him since the other night he's not answering the phone or anything. I'm starting to get worried. I know since he's been going through therapy and stuff for his knees that he isn't doing much but, he should still be able to talk on the phone." I said into the phone.

"No, I haven't got shit to say to him. How could he beat that girl like that and not think anything was going to happen after-wards? He's gonna mess it all up. It was good of you to think on your toes with that bogus ass story."

I smiled at my father's encouraging words. My father never gave me the credit that I deserved when I did anything good. Even when I started dealing with Gully he wasn't happy about it but, I needed some kind of way to scratch my lady itch. Things started out as just a fuck and duck situation but, when my dad and Lester got me involved in this land scheme that they had going on I foolishly told them about Gully being into land acquisitions. If I didn't get into that office soon then Gully would figure out that the story about Lester being dead was a damn lie. He would also know the one thing that no one needed to catch wind of right now.

"Martina I have to go for a walk at least. This is some bullshit keeping me in the house like this. I told you I could've gone out of town until everything was done. You and your dad insisted on me staying around here and in this house."

"Lester, just give it a few days before you try to leave the house. Martina's gonna have to play the damsel in distress to get on Gully's good side. She just has to get to the safe and get the property deeds to the land. We've come too far for everything to get crossed up just because you want to go outside. You have to think about it. Just sit your ass down for a little longer," my dad fussed through the phone.

Lester rolled his eyes and walked back to his room.

"He's getting real antsy daddy. Between him and Blaine one of them is gonna mess all this up."

I let my mind wonder back to Blaine. He was already having a hard time because Max had left but, now he wasn't answering any calls or messages. I knew that he was gonna break soon if we didn't get our hands on that paperwork.

"Go by his place and see where his head is at. I would but with your mother leaving because according to her I'm in love with Lester still. I tried to tell her I just like variety that's all. Lester just stayed around longer than the others. She's said that she was going to leave before but, she never did because there was an image to uphold now that the image is shot to hell, she made good on her threat. I'm trying to get my mind together. Dealing with your brother isn't going to help that."

I rolled my eyes because the last thing I wanted to hear about was my dad's sex life.

"Daddy can we get to the problem at hand. Max isn't

answering any of the phone calls. He has the money with him. What are we gonna do when we don't get in contact with him again?"

"Maxwell isn't gonna turn his back on us because he knows that just because he's not connected to us in the conventional way that he can still be connected if someone searches hard enough. I was against putting the money in his hands in the first place. If he runs off then we will just have to deal with it. I doubt that Gully will be so willing to fall for the same shit again. Go ask your brother has he talked to Max. If that's his best friend they should talk to each other every day. It's bad enough that your mother left because she swears I'm doing something illegal even though she doesn't have proof."

"We are doing something illegal," I told him.

"Yeah, I know. Just go talk to your brother. Call me later," he told me then he ended the call.

Dad knew that Blaine was gay but, he didn't know that Blaine was married to Max. With everything going on I didn't need Dad finding out that piece of information yet. That would only cause more problems. I fixed a drink before I called Blaine. He was so deep in depression that talking to him was draining. I didn't give a shit about Grace or Gully at this point but, he still swore that Gully was still gonna come kill him. I tried to explain to him that if Gully left him alive then it was a good chance that he wasn't gonna bother him anymore. He just didn't want to hear what I had to say. I wasn't going to his house because I just didn't want to deal with the pain of seeing him in the state that he was in. I dialed his number half way wishing that he didn't answer the phone.

"Hey Martina," he answered sadly.

"Blaine Dad said he's been trying to talk to you. What's going on why are you not answering the phone?"

"Answer the phone for what exactly, Martina? He's a gay man living on the down low basically but, he wants to disown me his GAY SON. Please explain to me what he and I would have to talk about," he told me.

"You two just need to talk. Did you know Mom moved out?"

"So did Max."

"You and Max weren't married for as many years as mom and dad."

"What's that supposed to mean? Mom stayed married to him because of the money and status his name used to bring. He was connected to all this city officials due to his career and all that. She never loved him and he wasn't in love with her. Max and I have been in love with each other for as long as we've been together. Now because of the shit that you and dad have going on he left me."

If Max loved you, you would know that he's working with us and the real reason he left was for him not to get caught with us.

"Have you talked to Max since he left?" I asked hoping he had.

"No, he wouldn't answer the phone and when I called the last few times the number was disconnected," he told me.

"If you called and the number was disconnected why would you call again?"

"I don't have an answer for that. I just want all of this to be a bad dream. If I wouldn't have gone to that house that night none of this would be happening. Tick would be alive too," he said sniffling.

Him saying that Tick was dead got my attention quick as hell.

"How do you know Tick's dead?"

"His sister called me saying that he was found in the park dead. He wasn't shot or anything but, I know that there is some bullshit mixed in because there wasn't shit wrong with Tick. There's no way a healthy man can randomly die in a park out of nowhere. I know I'm next and I'm not gonna run. There ain't nothing left for me to live for anyway."

"Stop talking like that Blaine. You will make it out of this fine. There's no need for you to even think about dying your time isn't going to come 'til years from now. Believe me, you're going to find love again. It's gonna be better than ever."

I had to try to help any way I could. I should've been the one worried I had stolen money from Gully but, I wasn't worried because if he hadn't found out that everything I told him was nothing but lies then he probably would never find out. I just needed Blaine to act like he had a little bit of sense. It was wild how he wasn't in on the scheme but, he could be the one to fuck everything up. If he would've left Grace alone then Gully wouldn't have found out that we were brother and sister. The plan was to introduce Max to Gully as my long lost adoptive brother. Gully would've taken the explanation that I had laid out without too much push back. I had sat down and mapped out every instance that he may question. However, he never took the bait by agreeing to help. The more I thought about it was evident that Gully was up to something but, I didn't know what.

CHAPTER 9

Russ

We pulled up to the warehouse that Caretha was tied up in. I looked at Adrian and her crazy ass looked like she was excited to do some shit. I had to laugh at her because even though I was just getting used to the woman that she's become there was a small piece of me that thought she was just fronting about doing some damage to Caretha. Looking at her with her leg bouncing up and down, her eyes big as I've ever seen them and her not being able to be still showed me otherwise.

"Don't get in here and start smiling and shit. You're already acting like a little kid. You can't put fear in someone acting all happy and shit."

"I've read enough urban books and I watched enough hood movies on Amazon Prime to have a good idea of how this goes. I haven't done this before but, I'm not slow either. Just follow my lead and it'll be all good."

"Follow your lead huh?" I asked her.

"Just come on and watch your woman work," she said just before giving me a kiss before she got out of the car.

I adjusted my dick that was involuntarily moving before I got out to follow her. She knew I was watching her ass because she damn sure was swinging that motherfucker from side to side. She waited for me to open the door for her.

"Russ umm, you really brought your woman here with you, nigga?" My homie Tip asked.

We called that nigga Tip because he looked like he could be the rapper TI's brother. They were the same short ass height and everything. The only differences were the way he talked and that cut that TI had on his lip that nigga didn't have. It was crazy how many chic's he picked up in the club just off his looks. Most of the time they were too damn high or drunk to notice the differences when he started talking to them in the club. I don't remember a time when he left the club solo. It was a damn shame how much pussy that nigga got just because he looked like the nigga. Not to mention TI's ass is married. If they didn't care with a fake ass TI I can see why the real one is always caught up in some shit behind some outside pussy.

"Babe he looks like..," Adrian started to say but I cut her off.

"That nigga TI, yeah we know that's why we call his ass Tip. The nigga's real name starts with a Q or some shit like that. We've been calling him Tip for so long I doubt anybody remembers his government," I told her.

I walked over to where Caretha was looking at her made me want to slap the shit out of her. Her ankles were tied to the legs of the chair with some white rope. They had put cuffs on her hands and a piece of something in her mouth. She looked up when she saw my shoes in her line of sight. She had her head down as she cried. She started trying to talk but, I couldn't understand what she was talking about. I was about to ask her a question when Adrians fist came out of nowhere hitting Caretha on the left side of her face. The word damn filled the room as the three guys that were in there heard the same noise that I did when Adrians fist connected with Caretha's face.

"I can't believe you tried to get me arrested for some shit that you started. Then you have the nerve to hum at my nigga while I'm standing here," Adrian said before she hit her ass again.

Did she really just say hum? I'm gonna need to find out what kind of books her ass has been reading.

Instead of interfering I stepped back where the other guys were to observe.

"That's your woman?" The homie Coke asked as we watched Adrian punch Caretha a few more times. I nodded my head up and down confirming that she was my woman. "Damn do she got a sister? Shit she's your Bonnie for real out here. That's the type of shit I need," he continued chuckling.

I didn't answer him because he wasn't gonna keep talking about Adrian and looking at her like he wanted her to be his girl. He was gonna fuck around and be laid out on the floor next to Caretha. We continued to watch as Adrian went over to the table that was decorated with a ton of bizarre shit that could be used in street torture. She was looking at the table like she was a kid in a candy store. I would've never thought that this is where I would be. You wouldn't be able to convince me that I'd be standing here trying to mentally force my dick not to get any harder while I watch my future wife handle my ex fuck buddy.

"You thought you had all the answers huh?" Adrian asked Caretha.

I guess it took her a minute to realize that Caretha couldn't talk with the gag in her mouth. She took the gag off of her then stood in front of her looking down at her. "Speak ya mind bitch. You went through all of that shit for what? If I wouldn't have come back you would still be walking around here like you're his bottom bitch and proud of that shit. I'll never under-stand you pick me bitches. Y'all just take whatever a good piece of dick dishes out. Well, look how far it got your ass," Adrian said smiling.

"For you not to be concerned you damn sure are looking worried to me. If you think you got it like that then, why the hell am I here right now? You must be worried about something," Caretha said trying to get under Adrian's skin.

"Nah, I'm really not. It's just that I would like to ride my man's dick without your stalker ass peeping in the window. You've already proved that you can't survive without Russell in your life so I have to take your life," Adrian said. Caretha started laughing out of nowhere.

"You aren't gonna kill shit. Now, if Russ was standing here then I might be scared. Then again, I would just suck his dick to make him forget all about you."

Adrian smacked her ass with a big ass wrench. I didn't even see her pick up the damn thing off the table. This was some sexy shit to look at. Any nigga that I know will tell you that seeing a woman with painted nails holding a gun like she knows what to do with it is sexy. I can tell them that seeing your woman torture a bitch that can't let go will make a nigga want to fuck her right there. I was tired of trying to adjust my growing dick every two minutes. I needed to get inside Adrian like never before. This woman was driving me crazy.

"Are you sure you don't want to just leave town and never come back?" Adrian asked Caretha.

"I want to ride Russ's dick until he nuts all inside my pussy. Once I have his baby we'll name the baby Adrian," Caretha told her.

"Too bad, I would never name my child some ghetto ass shit like Caretha. Just like it's too bad you didn't say yes to moving out of town for the rest of your life. Since you can't stay away from Russell on your own we have to make other arrangements."

Adrian lifted the gun and sent two shots into Caretha's fore-head. It was quiet for a few minutes as Adrian stood there looking at Caretha's body with her gun at her side. I walked over to her slowly taking the gun out of her hand. I put it on the table knowing that the fellas will get rid of everything later. There was something that I had to do first. I went back over to Adrian.

"Are you okay? I'm saying how are you feeling about all this?" I asked.

"I'm hungry," she replied.

I shook my head at her as I got down on one knee.

"Yeah, he just as crazy as her ass is," one of the guys said.

"Nigga don't do it if you're gonna cheat. We all know what she's capable of. Think about that shit thoroughly nigga," another guy said.

"Adrian I never thought you would come back into my life. I wished and prayed that you would but, I never thought the shit would happen. When you did it made my world complete well, partially anyway. After I knock you up with a couple of kids my life will be dope as fuck. I need you to marry my ass first though. What you gonna do?" I asked her.

"Yes, Russell, I'll marry you," she answered.

"Y'all clean this shit up. I got something to handle in the office right quick. When y'all get done just leave," I told the guys as I took Adrians hand and let her to the office with the one way windows. I was laughing at Gully when he was adamant about putting them in here but, I was gonna put these bad boys to use right now.

"Russell why are we up here we can just go to the house?"

"Nah, that's gonna take too long. Take that shit off," I told her as I took my clothes off.

"What if they hear us?"

"They just saw you kill a chic and you're worried about if they hear you fucking?" I asked her.

"You know what I'm saying."

"Yeah, I hear you but, you took those damn clothes off didn't you."

I pulled her close to me as I leaned against the desk. I lifter her left leg so I could watch my dick slide in her pussy. She inhaled as I slid in until she couldn't anymore. I watched as she closed her eyes and bit her bottom lip. I spun her around so that she was now bent over in front of me. My hands gripped her waist and I started fucking her harder.

"Russell, oh shit, Russell."

"Yell my damn name Adrian. Let them mother fuckers know who's pussy this is."

I continued to crash my dick into her. Just knowing that she would kill for me hand me hornier than I had ever been before.

"Yes, baby. Fuck me harder. Give it to me," she moaned.

I could feel my orgasm reaching it's peak. I slapped her ass twice and seeing her ass jiggle sent me over the edge.

"Ahhhhhhh shit Adrian. Got damn it woman I fucking love you," I said as I shot her womb up with our future child. We came at the same time until we collapse right there on the floor. Our breathing was labored, our naked asses were in shock from the coldness of the floor but, in our eyes there was nothing that could more romantic right now.

CHAPTER 10

Grace

I was still hearing Gully admit that he intentionally got me pregnant. When I first heard him I was pissed. Now that a day or two has passed I'm not mad anymore. In a weird twisted way I wanted to thank him. I just couldn't find the words. Instead of walking in the room where he was and telling him I was sitting in another room being stubborn.

"Why are you in here and he's answering the door like he lost his damn dog?" Auntie GiGi came in talking loud as ever.

"We had an argument. What are you doing here?"

"I came to see about you since your phone keeps going to voicemail. I thought y'all were over here working on another baby until he opened the door. If you two spent as much time fucking as y'all do trying to push each other away you'd be pregnant right now."

"Auntie he told me that he knocked me up on purpose," I told her.

She looked around like she was looking for something then she looked back at me.

"Okay, so what's the problem. If you slide on that man's dick knowing he didn't have a condom on then you got yourself knocked up."

"I guess you're right but, it would be my bad luck that I got knocked up the first time we did something with each other. That was the most ghetto thing I've ever done getting knocked up during a one night stand," I said rolling my eyes.

"Would it have been less ghetto if you got knocked up by a man that you were with forever and a day but, didn't love? It doesn't matter what the outside circumstances are whenever a baby is made it's a miracle. You can't say that you're worse off than you were before that night. I know that you can't."

"Auntie GiGi this isn't a movie or a book this is my life. I can't trust him if he knocked me up on purpose," I explained.

I know she was all for Germain and I getting together but, there was no way that she could dress this up to make him look good. She wasn't gonna stop trying though. I knew it just like I knew what my name was. This was gonna be a long visit I know that for sure.

"Chile boo, now if he would've knocked you upside your head I would agree with you. You can't say all that and he has taken care of you this entire time. Shit I offered for you to come to my house but, he shut that all the way down. You need to get your ass up and go talk to him. You don't want him out of your life just like he doesn't want you out of his. I don't understand y'all. You're wasting all this time life is too short for all these games. Adrian ain't waste no time getting her man back but, here you are sitting here making up shit in your head," she told me.

Her phone went off. I watched as she looked down at it, started smiling, licked her lips, typed a few words then put the phone back in her purse.

"Ummm who was that?" I asked her.

"My man. Yes, unlike you I do have one. Don't try to get all in my business either."

"Who is this man? Where did you meet him? How old is he?" I asked.

"Gully's sexy ass is right down there. Go down there and sit on his lap, hunch on the man let him know you appreciate his sexy ass."

"Umm I asked you some questions."

"I know, I heard them but, guess what I'm not telling you shit about my man until you admit and start acting like you have one. "

"Germain and I have not established a relationship," I told her.

"Why is that?" Germain asked.

I was so into trying to find out who Auntie GiGi was texting that I didn't notice that he was standing in the doorway. His eyes were on me

"Yeah Grace why is that?" Auntie GiGi chimed in with a smirk on her face. I rolled my eyes at her. "Roll them again I dare ya."

"Germain, just because you were determined to make me your baby mama doesn't mean that you want me as your girlfriend."

"You are as hard headed as a kid doing the fruit snacks challenge. I'll tell you what if you want to go home then by all means do you baby girl. I was gonna keep you here to show you that I love you and it had nothing to do with the baby but, since you're not hearing me get your shit and go. I won't call or bother you again. I'm too much of a sexy mother fucker and a boss to keep trying to show you some shit that you don't want to see. Just a heads up ya boy Blaine is still out there so you're gonna need to keep ya head on a swivel."

I sat there on the bed watching with my mouth open as he walked out of the room. The feeling of Auntie GiGi staring at me let me know not to look her way at all. I took a deep breath I swung my feet onto the floor.

"Do you want me to call in your order or do you want to order online?" Auntie GiGi asked confusing the fuck out of me.

"Huh?"

"Don't sit there and act like you weren't sad that all that good human dick just walked out. I know you're gonna want something to at least try to replace it and him. The first step is going to the adult toy store to get the biggest dildo in the same complexion as Gully's baby arm that he has in his pants. If not you're gonna be needing carpal tunnel surgery in a couple of months," she said with a straight face.

"Auntie can you call Rick to see if he can help me get what things I do have here so I can take them back to my place."

"I'm not giving you any more help or advice after this. You're wrong as hell for letting him walk out like that. You'll understand whenever the Lord creeps into your dreams and shows you something to make you realize that you're making the biggest mistake of your life. Mark my words you will regret this day."

)()()()()(

7 Months Later

I stood in my office looking at the lounge floor. I was lost in my thoughts *again* about the last day that I had seen Gully. Yes, his ass was Gully straight like that. Germain was the loving man that doted on me. He may have even loved me but, I found myself flip flopping about if he did or didn't love me daily. *Mark my words you will regret this day.* Auntie GiGi's words echoed in my head as they did often. When I left his house that day I was angry and frustrated at everything except the person I should have held those emotions for which was me. The whole time I was the problem. Me and my inability to allow myself to love or be loved. I knew what the problem was and I had taken time to take a self-inventory of myself. I guess you could say I was working on me. The problem was there wasn't a need for me to work on shit. Gully had made it painfully clear that he wasn't fucking with me in any way possible. I refused to ask Russ or anyone else about him. I'm sure Auntie GiGi was still talking to her *nephew* on the regular. Rick had come to DJ a few times but, I wasn't asking him shit either. I had seen the apartments that his company had built. They had other constructions going up everywhere. I had taken Adrian's advice and started dating. There was no sex involved just a few dinners here and there. There wasn't anyone challenging enough for me though. They were all too invested in themselves, were constantly reminding me of what material things they had or were just uninteresting as fuck. Most of all I just missed Gully.

Glancing at the clock on the wall I was happy as hell it was close to closing time. I was tired, unfocused, irritated, and horny as fuck tonight. I had been thinking of Gully more than usual lately. When I first left his house it was bad like I almost went crazy type of bad. Eventually Adrian came over laid my ass out and whipped me into shape. From then on I've been smiling, laughing, talking, and all that shit but, in reality I'm just going through the motions. I was going out with men that I knew wouldn't get past the first date. I seriously had it bad for Gully and there wasn't shit I could do about it to make it better.

I needed to at least hear his voice. I picked up my phone to play one of the voicemails that I had received from him before we went our separate ways. Whenever he got on my mind heavy like he is now I would listen to the old voicemails. That way it will stop me from going to his house and try to convince him that we should get back together. To put it mildly I was a hot ass mess behind our break-up. My heart ached for him but, my mind was too prideful to go back to him. I can't even remember what the argument was about that got me here. I was knocked off my square in a major way.

"Boss lady, we have another full house and it seems that we sold out of those one night-stand cigars among some others. I put the order in the day after tomorrow do you want me to order double what we ordered last month?" My assistant asked me.

I ordered those just to gift Germain with a box. I didn't think that other customers would buy them up like they are. I was thinking about discontinuing them all together. Every time someone said the name of the cigars I thought about Gully. I came to work to get him off my mind not think about him more. I don't know who I thought I was kidding. I came to work and would think of him as soon as I walked in the door. The bar would remind me of the night we shared when we created our little angel. The bottles of 1738 behind the bar made me think of him pouring it all over me just to lick it off. Germain and I weren't together long but, we damn sure made a lifetime of memories for me to hold on to.

ully

I was sitting in my office trying to focus on the potential land purchases and upcoming building projects but, I was just looking busy. I hadn't been able to function since the day that Grace left my house.

Troll: *She's on a date with some corny looking dude.*

Me: *Is she having a good time?*

Troll: *Nah not from what I see. Dude might think otherwise. I'm sitting across from them. He hasn't stopped talking about all the shit he has like boats and shit. She ain't feeling him at all.*

Me: *cool*

Troll: *Ya ass is terrible*

I laughed as I put the phone down on my desk. I shook my head trying to understand where the hell Grace's head was at. There's no way she can even have a small interest in the clowns that she started goin on dates with. There was knock at the door.

"Come in."

"We have a problem with some of the properties that were purchased by us in the last two months," Scarlet said with a look I couldn't quite read on her face.

I sat up in my chair contemplated if I wanted to know what she was about to say. I knew just by looking at her that I wasn't going to like it.

"What's going on?"

"I think I can explain it better if you come in the conference room. I've been in there since yesterday trying to connect the dots."

I got up to follow her out of my office. She was speed walking which only let me know that this was way too damn serious. I tried to run different scenarios through my mind as we arrived to the conference room but, nothing that I came up with made any sense. When I walked in the office there were pictures of four pieces of land on the board with words in all different colors. There was one name at the bottom though that was circled in red... Martina.

"What is going on?" I asked.

"The bank called me about a discrepancy in an account number the other day. It wasn't one of our accounts but, it was one that we were transferring payment to for land. In the time that I've been here there's never been a discrepancy with one number so that made me go back and look into the purchases that we executed in the past four months. I researched the buyers and even called them to make sure that the payment was made or to see if there were any problems with the transactions. Everything checked out but these four. When I went to call the numbers listed as the sellers, or institutions that held the property deeds all of the numbers were disconnected.

"When I started pulling dates and emails of all the correspondences dealing with these properties I noticed that all the emails were similar. When I did the email look up they all belonged to one person," she said as she crossed her arms and looked at me.

"Martina?"

"Yep that skanky whorish woman thought she had all the sense in the world but she don't. That ugly ass heffa, I told you a long time ago there was something about that gremlin that I didn't like."

"Scarlet can we focus on the situation at hand. Why is she connected to all of these properties? From what I see there aren't in a prime location or anything they're just pieces of land. What was her end goal?"

"Oh I didn't get to the good part. The best part of all of this is that not only did she not have the rights to the land but, the land was never for sale in the first place. That got me to thinking she had to have someone down at the city to show that this land was for sale. Every document we have regarding the sale of the land from the city has one signature on them. The name on all the notarized paperwork is Maxwell Jamison," she said with a smile that made me laugh. She was really excited at her detective work.

"Who is he?"

"Martina's brother-in-law according to the court records that I saw," she told me.

I stood to my feet.

"What about the money that we paid for the land?" I asked.

"I'm in the process of working with the banks to see how much of it that we can recoup. I'm hoping for us to recoup at least half but we'll see. I have the address for the Jamison guy and Martina's information in this folder. I can't believe that scoundrel thought she was going to get away with this shit.

Excuse my language but, she gets on my damn nerves. Oh yeah, I found out that her parents and old ass husband are flat broke. I'm sure she thought this money was gonna help them get back on track."

"She didn't know I have 004 from MI6 on my team. You done found out more than *James Bond* does in his movies."

"Oh hush you know I think of you as one of my own. I couldn't protect my son over in Afghanistan but I'll be damned if I don't try to protect you. All the information is right there in the folder. The ball is in your court now. You can turn the scoundrel in or make her a missing person's file I'll leave all that up to you."

"You can take off for the rest of the week," I told her.

"And do what? I'll come in I may get with my friends that are still living on go play bingo or something but, I'll be here," she told me.

When she left from the conference room I made a phone call.

"What's the play?" He answered.

"I need you to go out of town to pick someone up for me. Make it a quiet pick up," I replied.

"Cool send me the info."

I ended the call then sent him the address of Maxwell Jamison. I knew it was going to take a few days to get him here where I needed him to be but that just gave me time to plan some shit.

"What's the deal with Scarlet? She's at her desk mumbling and shit. "What did you do?" Russ asked when he walked in.

"It wasn't me this time man. Look at this shit," I told him as I handed him the folder that Scarlet had given to me. I watched as his face got more balled up the more that he read.

"This bitch man, a million fucking dollars though. Please tell me you gonna gut her ass man. She's just fucking trifling for this shit. Her and her gay ass family, all them mother fuckers need to go. I'm not talking about jail either. Like what the fuck, yo. Just let me know what the move is me and Adrian will be there."

"Adrian?"

"Yeah, I've been so wrapped up in her ass. I can't get enough of her gangsta boo ass. My baby held it down man. This all went down a while back. She took Caretha out at the warehouse. That was the sexiest shit I've ever seen in my life. She had my dick harder than it was when I would go to the strip club looking at all the acrobatic naked bitches. I took her ass in the office and fucked the shit out of her. I hope I already knocked her ass up. I've been trying since we got back together. I think something's wrong with my dick. If she doesn't comeback here pregnant I'm gonna need you to recommend me to a dick doctor. I already made up my mind that the baby's nickname is gonna be 'killa'," he said laughing.

"Killa, nigga really?

"Hell yeah that shit sound dope as fuck. I came up here because I need you to be my best man. Adrian and I are flying to Vegas to get married and fuck and shit like that."

"I'm there can I bring a guest? Hold up nigga I thought y'all were going down to the justice of the peace or some shit the way you were talking about marrying her a few months ago?" I asked.

"Shit, if it was up to me we would've been married. Adrian wants to do some big shit in Vegas at night and some more bullshit that doesn't have shit to do with me. I told her to just let me know the price and the time. She can do what the fuck she wants. It ain't like we're gonna do this shit again anyway. Ain't no divorce going on around here," he said.

"Like I said I'll be there with some big booty bitch that I can squeeze on and shit," I said with a mischievous smile.

He looked at me and started laughing. He knew I was only asking because I was gonna do some shit to piss off Grace.

"All I'm gonna say is when she beats your ass and whoever it is that you bring with you; I'm not breaking up shit. Adrian ain't getting in y'all's shit either. You need to just go over there and tell her what the deal is. You love her ass and you're taking out the niggas that you think she might like." I looked up at him. I didn't think he knew about my pet project. "Yeah, nigga I know all about the shit you got Troll doing for you. The shit is stalkerish as fuck and you know it. Why the fuck you waiting on snatching her ass up?"

"I can't look her in the face until I handle Blaine's ass. Now that I know what the real scam was I might just go talk to her when I handle them though," I told him.

Now that my gut instincts were telling me that I found out what I wanted to know I could kill them without anything coming up that I didn't know about. Once the Max guy comes to town there was gonna be a drop in the population.

"You're grown and I'll have your back in everything except Grace kicking your ass. That's that domestic shit and I don't do domestic shit. Let me get out of here and go fuck on Adrian some more. I'll hit you up with the details and shit in a couple of days."

He dapped me up before leaving. I was left there standing in the conference room looking at all the shit that Scarlet laid out. Shaking my head I should've known that there was more to it than that bullshit ass story she was trying to kick to me. My boy had already told me that Lester wasn't dead. No one had seen him but, it was clear he wasn't dead. Now I just needed to get all of them in one spot so they could start telling on each other and shit. I know Martina isn't the type to stand ten toes down for anyone regardless of the relationship. Now that I had all the answers I just needed for all the chips to fall into place. Once this shit was done I was definitely going to get my woman back.

CHAPTER 12

ully

I was sitting in the back of the restaurant sipping on some *Don Julio* and watching. I was watching Martina, Lester, and her dad have dinner. They were sitting and talking to Lester. Yes, the Lester that was supposed to be dead and buried under the apartment building that my company built. Neither of them knew that I knew that Lester wasn't dead or that I had seen the paperwork that was in my office that Martina was trying to get her damn hands on. I should've known the sneaky bitch was going to lie herself deeper in the hole she was gonna be buried in along with her brother and father.

After Grace left my house that night. I made a few calls to ensure that she was okay and not in any danger. I told her about Blaine still being out there because, I needed her to think she was alone. I would never leave her out here hanging like that. I meant what I said when I told her that she was always going to be my *baby mama*. She didn't know that I knew about each and every so-called date that she was going on. I knew about all the late night phone calls with niggas that were no longer breathing. It was gonna be my little secret that most of the mother fuckers that she went out with didn't call her back afterwards because they didn't have phones in heaven or hell.

I knew she was going through hell right now but, I needed her to understand that we belonged together and the best way to make her realize that was for us to *break-up*. There were nights I went and slept in her spare room and her ass never knew. It was the craziest thing because a few nights I just knew she was gonna come busting in the room with a frying pan or something. She never did I would hear her walking around, even a few phone conversations. I got a key to her house from Auntie GiGi, she was my homie for life. She knew that Grace and I belonged together so she would do anything to help make that happen.

"Would you like to have a refill on your drink?" The waitress asked pulling me out of my thoughts.

"Nah, unless I call you over here for something. I'm good on whatever it is you want to offer. Just let me be and I'll leave you a tip when I leave here," I told her.

I wasn't trying to sound harsh but I wanted her to leave my ass alone. She was shocked by my words but, she left so my mission was accomplished. I turned back over to the three stooges. It was fucked up that I couldn't just kill their asses like I wanted to all those months ago. I never thought it would take all this time to put the puzzle pieces together. I knew there was a nagging in my gut for a reason that night I went to the parents house. Now that I knew this was all just some scheme to use my company as a decoy so they could embezzle money from Lester's company I wouldn't have let Martina past the lobby of the building. It was a blessing for me that my secretary was more like a nosey mother. She saved the company and didn't even understand the severity of what she told me. I watched as they sat there laughing and joking like they hadn't stolen money from my black ass.

Quell: *The van is out back*

Me: *Okay I'm about to get this show rolling. Make sure everybody is in place*

Quell: *Word*

I drank the rest of the *Don Julio* and headed to their table. They were so deep in their conversation that I stood there for almost a minute before they looked up at me.

"Lester, you sure do have a lot of color in your complexion for a dead mother fucker," I said with smile.

"Gully it sure is good to see you," Martina said.

"I'll see if you still feel that way in about an hour. We have some things to discuss so if you all would be so kind as to walk out back with me I would appreciate it. I'm just saying it's the least that you could do being that you stole all that fucking money from me. I have guys posted up in this mother fucker so don't get any bright ideas about running and screaming or no shit like that."

Martina looked like she was ready to pass out while her dad and dead husband just looked constipated in the face. They all stood and started walking to the back door as I instructed them. Her dad was looking around trying to figure out why no-one had said anything about us walking to the back door instead of the front.

"Gully, you have to understand that I had no choice. I had to do this because it wasn't like you would've cared if I told you that my family including my husband and I were flat broke. You wouldn't have offered me any money or a job," Martina said as they got in the Van.

I chose not to respond to her dumb ass. She thought that by

pleading her case it was going to change my mind about killing them. The painful reality was that the more she talked the more I wanted to kill her. Her and her family's bullshit was hindering my happiness. The fact that her family being broke didn't have one damn thing to do with me. I didn't help them get broke so why would they feel like I needed to help them get more money. The shit they did was downright disrespectful. She kept talking while I tuned her ass out. It was either tune her out or punch her in the face. I didn't want to hit her just yet. I needed to see the reaction on all of their faces when they see my surprise. The van stopped and the side door opened. We hadn't blindfolded them or gagged them yet so when Martina saw the warehouse she started crying.

"I don't understand what's going on here," Lester said as he walked his old ass into the door of the warehouse.

"They're gonna kill us! We're not gonna live past tonight. We don't even have the money and we're gonna die!" Martina yelled.

The guys finally got the three of them tied up by their wrists and ankles. Now it was time for the two surprise pieces to come in. I gave the head nod and the guys brought in Blaine and Max. When the three stooges saw both Blaine and Max their faces were coated with looks of surprise.

"Why are you guys here? Gully your beef is with me not them. You can let them go first then handle me as you see fit," Blaine said as he was tied down.

I sat back waited for him and Max to be tied down completely before I said what I had to say. It was clear that everyone knew why they were here except Blaine. He was in the dark but, I was about to shed some light on things before I got to plucking them off.

"They say when a person dies that if they die in a state of confusion or disarray that the soul will remain in that state after death. Blaine I said that because, you're the only one here who doesn't know what the hell is going on," I said.

"I know that you're gonna kill me because of me making Grace lose the baby. I'm the one that did that but, no one else here is responsible for that. I knew you were coming for me that's why I didn't run. I let Max leave because he has nothing to do with this. I know that you helped get rid of the body. Being that Lester's here I don't know what the hell we buried that night. None of this is making sense." Blaine pleaded.

"Max is that true? You're here all because of some mistake? All you did was get rid of the so-called body, is that all?" I asked.

The way they all were looking guilty except for Lester was hilarious.

"I tried to tell you to leave Grace alone. You just had to go and fuck with her and mess everything up. If you wouldn't have done that none of us would be here. You messed up things that were in motion even when you had no idea what was going on. Of course we didn't bury Lester if he's sitting right there get a fucking grip. You wanna know what we buried that night? We buried some weights and sand bags wrapped in a few rugs that's what you buried. You never needed to know that if you would have kept your hands off Grace. When you put your hands on her you put this shit here in motion. You were never supposed to be involved in any of this," Max said shaking his head.

"So all that shit you said was all lies. You lied about every fucking thing. Before you left you threw that in my face like you burying him was gonna get you in trouble. You knew what was going on all along. How could you do this to me? You did this to us. I can't believe I loved you. You didn't give a shit about me," Blaine cried.

"Blaine you were too busy trying to please your parents to ever pay any attention to me. I was on my way out of the door until your sister came to me with her fantastic plan. I saw an opportunity to make some money and leave you with your backwards ass family. Who wouldn't take the chance?" Max said in a nonchalant tone.

Max was the only one here that wasn't crying or upset. I think he was mad that we found him more than anything else. Blaine was looking around at his people confused.

"Blaine you're in a room with nothing but liars. Max is your husband right or is he the wife? Nah, don't answer that. What you don't know is everyone else here worked together to steal over a million dollars from me," I paused to let that sink in.

"What is he talking about? Max you didn't tell me anything about a scheme. You were acting like you didn't know any of my family besides Martina? You already knew my father? What is really going on?" Blaine asked.

"Max you never told me that you were married to my son. All this time you were my son-in-law and never thought to say anything to me let me know who you were. I can't believe you," the dad said.

"What can't you believe? It's not like I have a daughter I can get him to marry and still fuck him behind closed doors. You fucking hypocrite! I fucking hate you!" Blaine said.

"That was a low blow Blaine," Martina said.

"Oh and having my husband mixed up in your twisted ass scheme is the high road? I'm just asking because both of you bitches are as low as they come. You're my damn sister we're supposed to look out for each other. Max is my husband but, I guess I was sleeping with the fucking enemy," Blaine continued.

It was clear that since he had come out to his family he wasn't hiding anything about his sexuality. He was moving that neck and blinking his eyes all fast and shit like he was a chic from the ratchet ass projects. I think if he wasn't tied up he would've tried to fight both of them.

"YO! That's not what we're here for. The subject at hand is the whereabouts of my money," I said looking directly at Max.

"Oh that's why your disloyal ass left so quick because you had the fucking money already. Shoot his ass first Gully I can't believe I've been home crying about what I did thinking that's what broke us up. It was you the whole fucking time. I can't believe you did this shit."

Blaine was too worried about his hurt feelings that he didn't see me pull out my gun. I sent two shots to his head. I thought about letting him keep living but, there were two things against him. The first was that he had been living too damn long as it was. The second was that voice of his was fucking annoying. He needed to use the seen and not heard method that I heard so much about coming up in the game. The logic behind it was that as long as you are present but, not attracting attention to yourself you could find out a lot more than you could if you were being a part of the chaos that surrounds you.

Lester started turning colors then, he appeared to pass out in his chair. *I just saved a bullet.* I shook my head because for a man that was involved with the two people next to him they didn't even flinch. Where was the love?

"Where is the money Maxwell?" I asked calling him by his real name.

"I already gave the account information to the guy that brought me here. I thought it would help me live. I figured the money was all you wanted," Max told me.

"It's not about the money it's about the disrespect," I told him.

I looked at the guy that picked him up and he responded by giving me a head nod. I knew then that the info Max provided checked out.

"Thank you for your co-operation," I said before lifting the gun and putting one in his head.

Martina jumped while her father shook his head. She was crying but, her father wasn't.

"Germain, don't do this! Germain, please don't do this?" She begged.

"I told you not to call me Germain," I told her before shooting her in the head. Her father looked at her slumped in the chair beside him. One tear fell from his eye but, he didn't beg for his life verbally. I sent a shot to his heart causing him to slump like the rest. I left the gun on the table and walked out while the guys went into clean up mode. I felt that a weight had been lifted. Now that they were all done for it was time for me to go get my woman back with her stubborn, hard headed ass. First I was going home to get me some sleep because I was mother fucking tired.

race

Two Weeks Later

I was enjoying time with my best friend helping her put the finishing touches on her wedding. She was so excited and I was just as excited for her. For her to be getting married to the only man that she ever loved was a true hood fairytale. Seeing her so happy made me forget about the loneliness that I was experiencing and the constant wet dreams about a man that I'll never feel again. My heart ached but, for right now this girl's time wasn't about me.

"I think it would be classy for everyone to throw rose petals instead of bird seeds or blowing bubbles. It may be all those times we used to watch *Coming To America* that helps me come to that conclusion. I always thought that walking on rose petals was gangsta. It was solidified when I found out how much them mother fuckers cost," she said laughing.

I laughed at her because that was one of the movies that we never got tired of watching back in the day. There were a bunch of them that were on the list but, that one was definitely high on the list. We knew every line and laughed like we didn't know the whole movie backwards and forwards. Those were the good old days. At least for me they were good. I didn't have to worry about getting my heart ripped out from my chest. I understand that was a bad time for Adrian but, it just prepared her for him to come back into her life permanently. That was some shit that we see on those bullshit ass prime movies where the chic always gets the happy ending. There wasn't a happy ending for me but, I refuse to be bitter with my sister/friend she deserved all the happiness that she was due to have. I was living through her vicariously until I find a man that I'm enough for.

"You're right but, I doubt if Russ will want a chubby guy standing up singing she's your queen to be while you come down the aisle." I said laughing.

"You play all day. I will have you know that he told me I could do what I wanted. All he wanted to know was the time, place, and where he was supposed to stand at. He told me that everything else was up to me. So if I want a chubby guy singing about how I'm his queen to be then that's what's gonna happen,"she said laughing.

"I hear you. Watch what I tell you. He's gonna lay your ass out if you put that shit in the wedding. That's even more ghetto than playing *lovers and friends* when you come down the aisle," I told her laughing so hard that I was holding my stomach.

"You make me sick. Since you're in such a good mood I need to tell you that Gully is the best man and from what I understand he's bringing a date," she told me killing my happiness instantly.

Before I could respond to her the doorbell rang. *Talk about saved by the bell.* I went to the door to see who it was. There was a white man dressed in a brown suit that he looked like he had on two days too long. I opened the door wondering what the hell had brought him to my door.

"Hello, how can I help you?" I asked.

"I'm looking for Grace Reynolds."

"You're looking at her. What brings you here?" I asked. He handed me a manila envelope.

"You've been served," he said before jogging to his car.

"What the fuck?" I asked as I closed the door.

"What's going on?" Adrian asked.

"I don't know some man dropped this off."

I sat on the couch opening the envelope. Inside of the manila envelope there was another smaller envelope that held a cover letter from a lawyers office. I read the cover letter but, it still didn't tell me why they were serving me with an envelope. I had never heard of this particular lawyer before. I pulled out the regular envelope that was inside of the bigger envelope. When I pulled out the letter inside of the smaller envelope there was a piece of paper that fell to the floor. Adrian picked it up before I did.

"Bitch this is a check for a hundred thousand dollars!" She screamed as she looked at the piece of paper. I unfolded the paper that the check was encased in. There was a handwritten letter.

Grace,

I know if you get this I have met my fate and retribution for the hideous act that I did to you. I will forever be sorry for taking my frustrations out on you that night. You didn't deserve it then and you will never do anything to deserve the type of pain that I dealt to you. You have always tried to help me even when I felt that I had everything under control. Please accept this money from my life insurance policy as a token of my regret.

Love Always, Blaine

"The money is from Blaine. He apologizes for beating me up and making me lose the baby," I told her as I sat on the couch.

"How do you feel about him sending you the money?"

"I doubt if I ever cash the money. I feel like it's some type of blood money. I would rather have my baby here with me. He's worse than his parents. He used to tell me how they felt like money could fix anything. Money can't bring my baby back so fuck him and this check," I told her.

To my surprise I didn't cry or feel any other emotion other then being mad that he tried to buy my forgiveness. I would never forgive him for what he's done. I understand that forgiveness is not for the person that did you wrong but, for you as a person. Maybe, one day years from now I'll be able to forgive but, not today.

"If you want to stop going over the wedding stuff we can start doing this in a few days or so," Adrian said.

"It's fine. You've been waiting for this day for almost a year now. I wouldn't be that cruel and make you put anything off pertaining to it for any more time than necessary. Let's get this done now because tomorrow we go to Auntie GiGi's for her little cookout."

"Yeah, I think she finally wants everyone to meet her little friend that's been putting that smile on her face. I'm surprised he's stuck around this long with her crazy behind," Adrian said laughing.

"Don't do my Auntie like that. She might seem a little special to some but, I love her just the way she is."

"Yup she's straight with no chaser all the way," Adrian added.

We laughed about Auntie GiGi some more before getting back to handling the wedding details. When we got to the wedding party I wasn't surprised that Germain was going to be the best man. That part I was expecting. It was just that seeing it on the paper made my heart skip a beat. The way Adrian had everything set up for the weekend Germain and I were going to be doing a lot of shit together. They were having a joint bachelor/bachelorette party so we were going to have to talk to each other and put our differences aside. I know that I can do that. When Adrian left that night I decided to call Germain so we wouldn't be uncomfortable with each other.

"Hello,"

Hearing his deep voice made me bite my bottom lip.

"Germain, this is Grace."

"Okay."

"I'm reaching out to you because Adrian and I were going over the details for the wedding next month. She has us doing a lot of shit together being that I'm the maid of Honor and you're the best man."

"Okay."

"I just want to be sure that there's no ill feelings between us. We have to at least try to get along for the weekend. I'm not going to ruin my best friend's wedding because you and I can't get along," I told him.

"How do you know so confidently that we can't get along?" He asked.

"What do you mean how do I know?"

"Exactly what the fuck I said. You walked out of my house that day and never looked back. You didn't even call me to tell me you made it home safe. You've been avoiding me like I have some type of disease that will kill you. You're going out on dates and shit. So again, how do you know that we can't get along? You haven't even tried to say hi to my ass like I did something to you other than try to take care of your stubborn ass. You made this phone call for what? I've never had a problem with you. So instead of calling me to project your bullshit onto me go look in the mirror and tell that shit to yourself. You're the only one with the damn problem Grace," he said.

"Germain, I don't have a problem with you."

"Tell that lie to someone who wants to hear it. I told you I loved you and instead of you trying to work out what we could've had you bounced."

"You told me to pack my shit and leave."

"I also told you a few times to throw that ass back harder. You only did that shit when you wanted to so that means you wanted to leave that night."

"I didn't want to leave."

"Yet, you not only left, you stayed gone, changed your number, and blocked me from the new number like I had the mother fucker in the first place."

"I didn't call you to argue."

"Who's fucking arguing? I'm stating facts beautiful. I have a question for you though."

"What's your question Germain?"

"Do you play with that pussy at night and scream my name like you did when I was so deep in that thing that you could feel the tip of my dick scratching your brain? Or do you have one of those dildo's that make all that damn noise so you can't concentrate on what I used to feel like?" He Asked.

I couldn't answer him. I wasn't going to give him the satisfaction of telling him the truth. Instead of staying on the phone to be sexually harassed by him I ended the call and blocked his number.

CHAPTER 14

$\mathcal{A}$untie GiGi

I'm introducing Hector to the family today. We've been together for almost a year now and that man has opened me up to a whole new world. He's so attentive and so damn sexy that we can't get enough of each other. He hasn't told me that he loved me with words yet but, I can feel the love whenever we're close to each other. When I told him about wanting to put this cookout together he insisted on me not working on anything today. After arguing we compromised. He was going to pay to have the cookout catered but, I was going to make the potato salad. There wasn't a chance in hell that I was gonna eat some potato salad that I didn't make. Everyone knows that potato salad can make or break a cookout well, it was that way in my family. Anyway so this was the first time that I was hosting a cookout but, didn't have shit to do.

"Do you need a refill on your wine love?" Hector asked me.

"No, I want to go in there and see what those folks are doing in my kitchen. I'm more stressed now than I was all the times I was the one preparing the food. If the food doesn't taste good you're gonna catch hell," I told him.

Hector started laughing at me just like he always does. No matter what I say he never gets upset. We don't argue but, when we get in that bedroom and he started folding my ass up in all kinds of ways he always tells me about my smart ass mouth.

"Did you tell Grace that Gully was going to be here?" He asked.

"No, this is my house they know not to start no shit in here. She needs to take her ass in one of the bedrooms and ride his dick if you ask me. I've never seen a woman run so much from a dick that she needed in her life before."

"I hope nothing pops off today," he told me.

"What kind of doctor are you that says pop off? Do you even know what that means?" I teased.

"I wasn't always a doctor. My family is sprinkled with dope pushers, drug addicts, shopaholics, and all that other shit that everyone's family has. I just stayed in school and raked up a bunch of fucking student loans that have to be paid back," he said with a smile.

I loved his smile.

"How much time do we have until everyone starts arriving?"

"About two hours, what's up?"

"You think we can get a few nuts in before that?" I asked.

"Well, that depends. You're not taking your ass in the house so you can start yelling at those people doing the job that they were paid to do. That means if you want me to work that pussy out we're gonna have to do it back here. Your two choices are for you to ride my dick here or in the pool," he told me.

Since that night we first met at the gas station we've been

constantly pushing the envelope in public. There was a rush of excitement mixed with the chance of getting caught that made the sex play or full blown sex more exhilarating.

"You know the windows are open. If I ride your dick right here then someone might see," I told him.

"Is that a problem for you today? Who gives a shit if they see us? I want them to see how my woman can ride the dick with so much passion and precision that they wish they had the energy that you have. You are the poster child for age doesn't mean shit. The fact that there's a twelve year difference between us doesn't mean a damn thing when you put that vintage pussy on me knocking me out every time. Bring that bomb ass pussy over here and knock my ass out," he said licking his lips.

I didn't waste any time as I hurriedly straddled his waist. He covered my butt cheeks with his large hands. He squeezed them a few times while kissing me all over my neck. Hector knew how to make me feel like I was the only woman in the world. I've felt things with him that I never thought a woman of my age would feel. He moved my bikini bottoms to the side. His swim trunks were pulled down just enough to get his dick to the wet entrance of my pussy. The feeling of my walls enveloping his shaft caused me to see stars in broad daylight.

"Georgette, baby damn you feel good," Hector moaned.

The constant balance of friction, pressure, and passion was enough to cause me to reach my climax in a matter of minutes. I yelled out in pleasure as I released all over him.

"Thank you for the quickie baby," I told him as I kissed him while getting off his lap.

"You think your slick get up so we can go to the pool house to get cleaned up. You still aren't going in the house to bother those people," he told me.

I laughed because I was definitely trying to see what the hell they were doing in my kitchen.

OOOOOO

After getting cleaned up and changing our clothes in the pool house it was time for the guests to start arriving. To my surprise everyone was no more than an hour and a half later than the time I told everyone to be here. Rick was set up playing the music and the party was now in full swing. I had introduced Hector to my brothers, nephew, Grace, Adrian, Russ, and Gully. They all were giving me funny looks but, I know that was because of how much younger he is than me. Nobody has said anything yet but, I know it's coming.

"Auntie GiGi when were you gonna tell me you were getting freaky with my doctor? I would've asked when you introduced us but, I didn't want to put him on the spot," Grace said.

"Ain't nobody worried about you putting anybody anywhere. You need to be trying to put it on Gully with his fine ass," I told her.

"Don't try to change the subject. I want to know about you and the doctor," she said crossing her arms across her chest.

"I met him before he became your doctor. I actually didn't know what exact hospital he worked at. That night I saw him I was surprised and shocked at the same time that's why I left the room."

"If I remember correctly he left a few minutes after you did. Did you two hook up that night?" She inquired.

"Yes we fucked in his office that night," I told her.

She gawked at me as she stopped in her tracks.

"Auntie GiGi I can't believe you," she said.

"Why not? I have never been scared of dick so I don't know what you're having a hard time believing. That man works me over every day." We both scanned the yard to see Russ, Gully, and Hector standing by the grill talking. I could see it all over her face that she misses and loves Gully. Her ass was just too fucking stubborn to admit it to herself or anyone else. "He still loves you. If you ask me he might love your annoying ass more."

"Annoying? Why are you calling me annoying?" She asked.

"Grace I love you just as much as I would my own child but you my darling are annoying as fuck. That man loves you and has killed for you but, you're out here going on dates with niggas that get on your nerves. Just so you can say you're not lonely. Let me tell you this and I pray that it stays in your head instead of going in one ear and out the other. You're gonna fuck around and lose him because your indecisive ass doesn't want to make a decision. Love isn't something you can control. The people you love are not to be controlled either. You're so scared of the unknown that you're going to miss out on someone that you KNOW loves you. Stop your bullshit before it's too late," I told her.

"He … He doesn't care like he did before. When I talked to him on the phone he didn't sound the same."

"Of course he didn't sound the same you had cut the man out of your life without one solid reason. Then you call him not because you realize you two belong together but, because you don't want the wedding to feel uncomfortable for y'all. You better be glad all he did was talk to you crazy. I know you may aspire to be like me when you're my age but, Hector is a one of a kind blessing made just for me. Like Gully is made for your annoying ass. Cut the bullshit and get your man back. I just might have to talk him into being in a polyamorous relationship with me and Hector if you don't," I told her with a sly smile.

"Auntie I just don't want to get hurt."

"Oh like you hurt him by leaving in the first place. I'm gonna help you out. I'm only helping because Hector gave me a bomb ass quickie before everyone got here. Go to your old room and I'll send Gully up there. Now if I send that man up there you have to promise me that you're gonna rectify this situation between y'all. If you're not done being stupid let me know now."

"I'm ready. I miss him so much Auntie it hurts," she pleaded.

"I know now take your dumb ass up to the room. He'll be up there in a few minutes."

I watched her walk into the house. I pray that she does the right thing because she's starting to make me think my brother must've dropped her a few times when she was younger. I slowly strolled over to where the guys were. They were talking about some team but, I had more important things to discuss.

"I hate to interrupt but, Gully can I speak with you for a moment?"

They all looked at each other with curious faces. I know they wanted to know what I wanted with Gully but, it wasn't my place to say anything in front of anyone. If he wanted them to know he would have to tell them.

"No, we didn't threaten your man if that's what you want to know," he said smiling.

Gully and I had gotten close with each other. He would call me on those nights that he wanted to go beat Grace's door down and take her back to his house in true cave man fashion. If Grace would just get out of her own way they could be so happy together.

"Grace is upstairs in her old room. I think it's time for you and her to talk. I'm saying laying it all on the line."

"The last time I laid everything on the line she packed her shit and left. I'm good on her," he said.

"You and I both know that your ass is nowhere near good. If you were good you wouldn't be calling me like a broken hearted lost puppy on the phone. I'm gonna tell you just like I told her. You both need to fix this. The only way that will be done is if you two stop with the bullshit. You and her both are being stubborn and annoying. Go talk to her and you two come out of that room as a couple or don't come out at all. I don't want to hear no excuses just get it done." I told him.

He gave me a kiss on the cheek and walked in the house. *Lord please help them fools get out of their own way.*

CHAPTER 15

ully

Auntie GiGi betta be glad that I love her like she's a blood relative. If I didn't think she would come looking for me if I walked out of the house instead of going to talk the Grace, I would leave. I knew deep down that Auntie was right because this shit had gone on long enough between Grace and I. I didn't want to force her to be with me. That was my biggest problem. I wanted her to come to me on her own. I guess this was as close as I was going to get to her coming to me. I walked into the room she was standing in front of the large window. The room overlooked the pool and backyard so I knew she was looking at everyone enjoy the party. I enjoyed the view of her body outlined by the setting sun. Licking my lips as my eyes caressed her body. For someone who had been through so much she looked delicious. Her ass looked to be a little fatter. *I wonder if it's still soft.*

"I didn't think she was going to get you up here," she told me.

"Auntie GiGi gave me an offer that I couldn't refuse."

"Is that offer the only reason why you came up here Germain?"

"What's going on Grace? She said that you had somethings to say to me. I'm here and listening," I told her.

I sat in the recliner chair that was facing the bed. I don't know why Grace thought that I was gonna be the one spilling feelings first. I wasn't gonna say a damn thing until she told me whatever it is that she had to get off her chest.

"I miss you. I apologize from the bottom of my heart for walking out that day. I should've known that you didn't really mean that you wanted me out. If we were going to be the couple that we had agreed upon we should've sat and talked about it. I dropped the ball on that in a major way. Then to make matters worse I've been avoiding you like the plague."

"Why would you do that? I never put you in a position to where you would be scared to be around me."

"I didn't avoid you because I was scared. I was scared but, not of you. I was scared of how you make me feel. I feel so exposed when I'm with you. I've been living life with a guard up for as long as I can remember. You come along and you see right through all of that. You make me feel naked."

I nodded my head as I listened to her.

"If you're scared of how you feel around me then, why are we in this room together?"

"We're here because no matter how unsure, scared, or exposed I feel around you. I would rather feel that if the only other choice I have is to be without you any longer. When I left you that day I figured that since we haven't been together long, it wouldn't be that bad trying to get over you. I was wrong because every night I reached out for you. I still have a few voicemails in my phone that you left. I listen to them sometimes just to hear your voice. I took two of your t-shirts when I left."

I laughed because I knew about the two shirts that she took. They were the two shirts that she used to walk around the house in. It got to the point that she wore them more than she did her pajamas. I didn't mind though because she looked cute in them.

"What else do you want out of this meeting Grace? Did you think that you coming clean about some things was going to make things go back to what they were before?"

I hope she didn't think getting back tight with me was going to be this easy. I was a damn boss and she had me out here hurting. That wasn't something that I could just wipe off and keep moving. She was straight tripping and I could tell that she was still holding shit back from me.

"Gully," she started but, I cut her off.

"Nah, you don't call me Gully. The only time you used that name was when you were mad about something. As far as I know I haven't done shit to piss you off so you need to change that. I need for you to put all your feelings and wants on the table. If you think we can ever go back to what we had before you can't be standing in my face holding shit back."

She shifted on her feet. I didn't care about her feeling uncomfortable. I've been uncomfortable since she walked out of my door. Hearing about the dates and shit all made me uncomfortable as fuck so fuck her being uncomfortable right now.

"You were right about everything. When you said that we belonged together and that you loved me. I was too wrapped up in my own pain and fears to see that you've been showing me the love that I was looking for the whole time. After I lost the baby, going back to the same house that I lost the baby in was fucking with my head. I should've told you but, I would see flashbacks of that night. There were times I would see me sitting in a puddle of blood. Then other times I would see Adrian knocked out because she was trying to defend me. It was hard on me mentally being there but, instead of talking to you about it, I tried to handle myself. Keeping everything bottled in because I didn't want to be a bother to anyone anymore. I had already leaned on you so much. I felt like I was losing my strength and independence by letting you be there for me. I felt like a useless woman because I was still hurting."

"Grace that's why I wanted to be with and around you. I didn't bring you to the house to just look at you. I'm not a woman so I can't tell you how you feel but, I know losing a baby hurts. I knew you were going to have a hard time. I wanted you with me because I feel guilty about how everything went down. If I would've been there or had some security Blaine wouldn't have gotten that close to you. We were both fighting battles when we should've been talking to each other instead. You weren't the only one to lose a baby. I wanted to be there for you."

"I don't know what made me think that you were only with me because of the tragedy. You were showing me your feelings before that happened. I didn't realize it until I was sitting home one night alone with popcorn and ice cream. When I figured it out I should've called you but, instead I went on dates with men that didn't matter. I was trying to replace you when all I had to do was call you. I wasted even more time convincing myself that us being separate was for the best. I've been nothing but, an asshole about this whole situation, I wouldn't blame you for not wanting to be with me now. I love you Germain. Being without you has been the worst time of my life. My father dying was my all-time worst point in my life. However, having our baby taken from us and us not being together is definitely in the second place."

She was standing in front of me now. I don't remember her walking over to me. My heart was beating and my dick was hard as a brick. Hearing her express to me that she loves me with so much emotion and conviction was music to my ears. She was looking down at me. Although, I was trying to remain indifferent about what she was saying. I took her hand and guided her to sit in my lap. I wiped her tears then kissed her lips. I couldn't resist it any longer. This woman had been away from me for months there's no way she can be this close to me without me kissing her.

"I just want to love you. Grace let me love you. Let me dry your tears and ease your fears. You can depend on me for anything, I put my word on that."

I stood up with her in my arms. Walking over to the bed I laid her down and hopped on her. I know we were making up but, my only mission right now was to get inside her. The firmness of my erection was starting to be painful. On second thought it could be the fact that I was finally back between her legs like I had been dreaming about.

"I love you Germain."

I heard her talking to me as I slid my pants down to my ankles. I pushed her bikini bottoms to the side. While I was doing that I could feel the dampness of the material from the wetness of her pussy. The pussy that I was about to invade with my hard dick. The pussy that could quench the thirst that I've had since the day she walked out of my house. Sliding inside her warm, sloppily wet hole that was still a tight fit around my shaft gave me the feeling of pure happiness because a nigga was finally back home.

As I reached the deepest part of her insides she dug her nails into my flesh. The pain of her breaking my skin only made this situation worse for her. Her causing me to be in pain gave me time to focus on something other than the immediate rush of cum that was building in around my balls. That only means that I could do more to her before I came inside her. I took my arm and lifted one of her legs so that I could suck on her toes as I pumped in and out of her. She tried to scoot away from me. I popped her thigh with my hand. I didn't have to tell her to keep her ass still. She knew what the deal was. She moaned out just like I knew she would. Grace was a true closet freak but, she swore that I was the only one that knew how to bring it out of her. I only did what felt right when we were together. The more she moaned the more I did. I just wanted her to let loose. It was a shame that my dick had to be digging deep in her for her to give me total control. I leaned over and squeezed her neck just enough to make her pussy start to grip my dick tighter. Her eyes rolled and she started to bite her bottom lip.

"That's right cum all over your dick Grace," I said as I pushed into her deeper and stronger than before.

"Ahhhh you're all in my throat Gully!" She screamed out.

She knew that shit set me off hearing her call me Gully. I leaned in closer to her ear.

"Since you want to play games with me, I'm gonna keep your ass up all night long," I whispered. I removed my hand from her neck and moved it down to her breast. I started playing with her nipple while I kissed on her neck and continued stroking her. Hearing her moan I started to pinch her nipple with my thumb and forefinger. "You want to fuck Gully?" I asked her as I increased the pressure of the pinch. Her mouth formed into a perfectly shaped replica of the letter O. I was now slamming into her while still pinching her nipple.

"Yes!!" She yelled out as I felt her orgasm coated my dick. When the orgasm subsided she closed her eyes while trying to catch her breath.

"Nah, we ain't taking no breaks tonight roll your ass over. Ass up, arch that back, find a pillow or something to hold on to because you gotta understand that you don't call me Gully. You gonna learn some shit tonight," I told her as I tapped her leg.

She looked tired already but, she could look that way all she wanted to. She could pass out if she wanted to I was still gonna fuck her until we both passed out. We had months to make up for and there's no time like the present to start the process.

CHAPTER 16

 race

Waking up in my old room in the arms of the man that I love was not the plan when I came to the cookout/pool party. My eyes had been open for almost twenty minutes now. I was just enjoying the feeling. After last night there were no more doubts in my mind about how much our souls were tied together. I'm sure that if I didn't get pregnant last night I would be soon. There was no way that I could ever walk away from this man again.

"If you have to piss you can get up. That's the only reason you'll be able to get up though. We just need to enjoy each other for the moment."

"How did you know I was up?"

"You're breathing pattern changed when you woke up. I've been up for at least an hour. I was watching you sleep for a while from the chair over there. I even snapped a few pictures."

"Oh gosh, I hope nothing was hanging out. Was my mouth open? I hope you didn't get close up on me," I told him.

Hearing that he was watching me had me self-conscious and embarrassed.

"I know you're not embarrassed by me watching you. You do realize that I've seen every part of your body on your good and bad days. I was the one cleaning you up when you were all messed up in the hospital. You should be good with me taking pictures of you sleeping. As for your question of if there was anything hanging out; I'm not telling you. Somethings are just for me to know," he said laughing.

"I could get used to this."

"You might as well. Later on today we need to decide on where we're going to live. Now, before you open your mouth with bullshit. I'm not sleeping another night without you next to me. We need to figure out the boundaries now before we start our day together. I don't want there to be any room for doubts or hesitations," he told me.

"I agree. How about we just go looking for a house of our own for us to start our forever together today?"

That made more sense to me than anything else. We could play house all we wanted to but, I would feel uncomfortable at his place. I'm sure he would feel some type of way staying with me

"That makes sense. Truthfully I've been working my ass off but, it was hard being in the house where you lost the baby at. The problem that I was dealing with was it was also the last place you were. I have memories of you being there. The times when Auntie GiGi came over talking her shit," he said laughing.

"That woman is a mess. She loves you though that's for sure. You can do no wrong in her eyes."

"Someone sounds jealous over there. It's not that I don't do any wrong It's just the fact that I own my shit. It doesn't matter if it's right or wrong. I'll never deny a damn thing that I've done. She's laid my ass out plenty of times behind you while we were apart. She kept me out of jail a few times."

"How did she keep you out of jail?"

"On those nights you called yourself going on a date I wanted to crash the date or break into your house and make you be with me. She would tell me to sit my ass down somewhere. She talked me down more than I care to share with you right now."

"How did you know about the dates?" I asked.

"I don't want you to get all pissed. You know how you get when you get your ass on your shoulders. I know about the dates because I had someone watching out for you. I only did it because Blaine and his twisted ass family were running around. Even with him saying he was sorry and all that other shit you never know. Once all that was done I pulled him off you two weeks later," he admitted.

"I know Blaine is dead. I never asked you about him because I already knew. I want to thank you for taking care of that for me. He left me some money," I told him.

"Who left you some money?" He asked sitting up in the bed.

"Blaine left me some money. The day that Adrian and I were going over the details for the wedding. Which just happens to be the day I called you, as well. We were sitting there going over the sitting arrangements when there was a knock at the door. When I opened it this guy hands me a big envelope telling me that I've been served and he leaves. Adrian and I both were curious to see what it was so we stopped what we were doing while I opened it. It turns out Blaine left me a letter apologizing with a check for a hundred thousand dollars. I didn't cash it because the money feels dirty. It's like he's paying for my forgiveness. You can have the check if you want."

He was perched on the bed silent as a church mouse. I could

see that he was thinking about what I said. I pondered if I should call him and tell him. The discontentment in his voice from the one conversation that we did have is what halted me from calling him again. I just couldn't handle it if he had the same tone as before. Now here I am nervous as hell that all the talking and love making that we just experienced would be all for nothing.

"You should deposit the check into a savings account," he told me.

"What? Why would I do that? I just told you that it feels like a pay off."

"Think about it Grace. You can deposit that money into the bank. Even if it feels like a pay-off to you; you can flip it and change the purpose of the money. You can let it sit in the bank and grow, you can give it to our future kids, or you can start a business with it. All I'm saying is that you shouldn't let it go to waste by not using it at all."

He could be on to something. Starting a business with it sounded good but, I don't know what kind of business I would start. The cigar lounge takes up enough of my time as it is. Business has been great since that opening night. I knew there was a need for a lounge of that type in that area but, I was pleasantly shocked by how good business was doing. We were on a constant upswing with people patronizing the place. I even launched an online ordering service a month ago that was getting more amounts of traffic than we anticipated.

"Grace," Germain called me getting my attention.

"I'm sorry. When you mentioned business it made me think of the cigar lounge. My mind drifted for a few minutes," I said with a chuckle.

"You have a couple of kinks you need to iron out with the online ordering that you set up. Even with those kinks you're shutting the whole cigar market down in the city," he told me.

"You ordered from my site?" I asked.

"How else would I know about the kinks? Hell yeah I've been ordering. I need to slow that shit down though because I have too many fucking cigars for someone who doesn't smoke those motherfuckers," he paused. After he skimmed my face he realized that I was shocked at what I just heard. "Grace you have to realize that even if we weren't together because you were being childish and annoying I still wanted to see you win. Yes, I've been ordering from your site. Yes, all the workers from my company are now regulars at the lounge because I rave about how good the drinks and prices on cigars are. No matter what I always want to see you win."

"Thank you, thank you, thank you!" I yelled out to show my elation at his confession. I wrapped my arms around his neck kissing him over and over on his cheek.

"Damn Grace. If all I have to do is send some people to the lounge and order a few cigars to get you that excited I'm never stopping," he said with laughter in his voice.

"Come on shake a leg so we can get the walk of shame over. I'm starving and you know Auntie is not going to leave here until she sees the two of us. I don't care what type of errands she has to run. It doesn't matter if she has a hair appointment either. She is gonna wait so she can go in on us when we walk out of her." I told him.

We got up to handle our hygiene then we headed down to the chamber of the unknown as we approached the living room. I could hear Auntie GiGi and Uncle Geon talking to each other. He must've stayed over last night too. As soon as we broke the corner they stopped talking and looked at us.

"Good morning," Germain and I said together.

"Morning? It ain't morning no damn more. It's two o'clock in the afternoon. I guess with all that fucking and hollering that was going on in that room you didn't have the energy to check the clock," Uncle Geon said as he leered at us.

"You need to go home if you're bothered by people fucking while you're under *my* roof. They were doing exactly what they needed to be doing. She was apologizing with her pussy and he was carrying out discipline with the dick that your annoying ass niece needed. Now everyone is all smiles and all is well in the hood. Don't you let him make you feel bad for busting it open for each other. He needs to find somebody to bust it open for him that ain't a damn Department of Social Services frequent flyer," Auntie GiGi said.

"Oh so since you went out here and found a young ass doctor that can bend you backwards you got so much to say about where my dick goes," Uncle Geon said thinking he was defending himself.

"You know damn well I've always had a lot to say about where your dick goes. All of y'all make constant poor and irrational dick decisions. I know daddy taught y'all better than that," she told him.

"I reckon you think I need to find a doctor to go be with like you huh," he said.

"Don't try to play me like that. It doesn't have to be a doctor or a lawyer. With your track record the supervisor of the fry station at *McDonald's* would be an upgrade for you."

"Kiss my ass GiGi."

"I'm not gonna do none of that for you. Take your ass in the projects I'm sure you'll run into someone that has kissed that mother fucker before. You don't have community dick you're walking around with project dick," she told him.

Germain and I couldn't hold it in anymore we both fell out laughing at these two. You would think that they were in a deep argument but, she was playing the game on her phone and he was flipping through the newspaper with the television on. Looking at them you would think they weren't insulting the hell out of each other. When you hear their words you would think they were fighting. This was my family and how they acted all the time. At the end of the day I wouldn't trade them for the world.

ully

After leaving Auntie GiGi's house I stopped by my place to take a shower and change. While I was taking my shower Grace stepped in behind me.

"I thought you were sore after all we've done."

"I'm not sore enough not to be horny. Just knowing that you're in here with all this water dripping all over your body. I couldn't resist," she told me.

She kissed me on my shoulder and I knew right then that we were going to be longer than the twenty minutes I had planned on. She kept kissing on my neck while she jerked me off from behind. I wanted to stop her in my head but, it was feeling too damn good to stop her.

"What are you doing woman?" I whispered.

"I'm just making my man feel good," she whispered back.

I don't know if it was the fact that the sound of the shower water hitting the floor and our body that made this whole scene erotic but, I shot my load right there in the shower. Once I got my release I turned around and made her bend over so that her hands are on the wall. I slid into her before I was sure she got her footing. I slithered in and out of her with the water falling on us and off of our bodies, that made me want to pound into her harder. I wanted to see how high I could make the water jump in the air off her body.

"I'm coming baby," I called out to her.

A few strokes later we came together. We were both soaking wet the water was now freezing cold. I helped her out before cutting the water off then, getting out myself. As we both dried off I couldn't remember a time that I was happier than I am right now.

"Now I'm sore enough not to be horny," she said laughing.

"You still have a pair of jeans and a shirt that you must've missed when you were packing. I'll pack a bag before we leave. I know that you don't want to stay here for the night. I get it but, I'm not sleeping without you," I told her.

"Thank you for understanding."

"I keep telling you that I'll do anything I can just so you can be okay."

We kissed some more then we got dressed. I had already called a realtor that I dealt with. She was the only one that I hadn't crossed a line with so she was the only choice. The other agents had either sucked my dick or gotten fucked by me. At the time I was single and willing to do whatever to make the deal get done. So that's why Tasha was the only agent for the task of the day. Tasha Thompson was thorough and efficient. She didn't play games about her money.

I had texted Tasha to let her know what we were looking for before we got in the shower. She had already sent a list of addresses and times for us to meet her by the time we made it out of the house. I texted her to let her know that we were on the way. I specifically told her that WE were on the way. I didn't need any miscommunications going on. I know that we've never crossed the line however, that doesn't guarantee that Tasha wasn't going to shoot her shot today. I was trying to shut all bullshit down before it even got started.

"How many properties have you bought with this chic?" Grace asked.

I shook my head because I knew exactly what was on her mind.

"Just ask it man and get the shit over with."

"Ask what Germain?"

"Since you want to play like you don't want to know if I've fucked Tasha in the past. I'll tell you. No, I haven't fucked or let her suck my dick. Is there anything else you want to know?" I asked.

"Why haven't you fucked her?"

"Shit if I know. We don't vibe that way. It's strictly business with Tasha you'll see what I'm saying. I would never put you in a position of doing business with anyone that I've been with sexually. Give a nigga more credit than that," I told her.

"I know but, I had to ask."

When we pulled up to the house Tasha was already there. She was parked in front of the house standing outside of her Land Rover talking on the phone.

"If we go in here and you don't like the house for any reason we're leaving and going to the next one. It's all about you today, I don't care if you don't like the knobs on the kitchen cabinets. If you don't like something we're leaving straight up. This is gonna be the house we raise our kids in so you gotta like the shit. You're the queen and this is part of your throne," I told her followed by giving her a kiss.

"Good Afternoon, are we ready to house shop?" Tasha asked excitedly.

That was one of the things that turned me all the way off about Tasha, She was too fucking happy all the damn time. I've never seen her without a smile or a hyper ass voice. The shit got on my nerves after a while but, that was one of the few things that I didn't like about Tasha.

"Yeah that's why we're here. Tasha this is my wife Grace. Grace this is Tasha. Tasha go ahead lead the way. I'm only here to sign on the dotted line. All decisions will be made my Grace she has the final say so on if we buy a house today or not."

"That's nice to know. Follow me so we can get this adventure on today. The weather is awesome for a day of house hunting don't you think? Nice to meet you by the way. You two make a fabulous couple. How long have you two been married?" She asked.

"Long enough. Y'all go 'head and look around. I'll be right here," I told them.

"Okay babe," Grace replied.

They started talking and took their asses down the hallway. They were down there for about fifteen minutes before they came back to where I was. I looked at Grace she shook her head from left to right and headed to the door. Tasha looked a little off but, instead of asking her what the hell was going on I headed outside to talk to Grace.

"What happened?" I asked.

"Are you sure you haven't shown your dick to her?"

"Yeah, why you ask me that?"

"She asked me what strip club did I work at. That was her first mistake then the bitch had the fucking audacity to point out that I didn't have a ring on. When I asked her why the fuck was she worried she tried to play it off like I was blind to shade she was throwing. That heifer may not have had you but, she damn sure wants your ass. I'm done with this house shopping shit. We can try again tomorrow. We can stay at my place or at a hotel. I don't care but, I know I need to get away from here before I get locked up today," Grace said then fast walked to the car.

I turned my black ass around and went to find Tasha in the house. Oh this bitch was gonna hear my got damn mouth. I could hear her on the phone.

"Yes, bitch a whole wife. I never even knew his fine ass had a girlfriend. All those times I was showing him properties I should've been throwing this pussy on him. I don't know who sis is but she damn sure secured the bag like a motherfucker." She listened to whatever the bird on the other end had to say before she started talking again. The dumb broad didn't even feel me standing behind her talking ass. "I didn't see a ring on so I may still have a chance to slide up in there. Let me get out of here so I can call my next client." She ended the call just to turn around and get stuck because I was standing in front of her now. "Oh Germain, I thought you had left."

"The name is Gully. Nah, I didn't leave yet because I gots nothing but time today. I always thought that you were a black woman out here about her business. The shit is disappointing as fuck just to find out you're a real life sac chasing bird with a career in these streets. How fucking dare you question my wife about anything? All you had to do was show her some fucking houses but, you couldn't do that shit right."

"I apologize if she felt offended by anything that I may have said."

"Fuck all that fake apology shit you're talking with your disrespectful ass. There ain't shit you and your overly renovated pussy can do for me. You will have a better chance of riding a cactus like a dick than you have of even seeing my shit. Lose my number Tasha because I already lost yours. If I find out your out here running your mouth about my wife and I, I promise you won't like me. That's a side of me you never want to see. Just so you won't be shocked when you get back to the office I'm calling the owner of the real estate office. You might want to start revising your resume. We all know how much money I spend with the firm. I highly doubt if they want to lose my patronage because of your bird like activities," I told her before leaving the house

To my surprise Grace didn't ask me what I said to Tasha when I got in the car. I drove straight to her place.

"I'm sorry about what happened."

"It ain't on you, all that was on her bird ass. I'm sorry for exposing you to her bird ass. We can go check out some places tomorrow. It ain't no thang to me baby."

"When we get in here we're not having sex,"she said laughing.

"Oh yeah, let's see how that goes for you," I told her as we got out of the car.

I could get used to this shit with Grace.

drian

"Best friend, you should've slapped that whore a couple of times. Ain't no way I wouldn't have put paws on her," I told Grace.

My friend was back smiling, walking around with that 'I got my man back' glow.

"You know Germain shut that whore down. We went looking for houses the next day. I hope we find one before we leave for the wedding next weekend."

"I hope you do too. I know how it is though. Okay so I have something tell you and you can't tell a damn soul. I'm saying not even Auntie GiGi."

"Oh shit, if you cheated on Russ I'm fucking you up. I'm not co-signing no flawed shit Adrian. That man loves you. This is so disappointing, just a damn shame."

"If you would shut up then I could tell you that I'm pregnant not that I'm cheating," I said cutting her off.

Her eyes got big, there was a huge smile that spread across her face and she stood to her feet.

"I'M GONNA BE AN AUNTIE!!" She yelled.

The entire food court area stopped to look at us.

"If you don't sit your extra ass down. You got all these people looking at us like we're crazy. You're gonna fuck around and we'll be trending on twitter or some shit," I told her.

"Oh my bad, I'm just so happy that I'm gonna be an auntie," she said dancing around in her seat like a child. "What did Russ say? I know he's happy as hell."

"I haven't told him."

"Why the fuck not? Adrian don't be on no bullshit tell the man. He might be like his friend and get you pregnant on purpose. His ass is just waiting on you to tell him watch what I tell you."

"Huh? What the hell are you talking about? You know what never mind I don't even want to know the details behind that comment. I'm sort of scared to tell him. What if he doesn't want a baby right now?" I told her.

I know that Russell loves me but, a baby is on a different level. What if we're not ready? What if we need more time to solidify the relationship before a baby comes?

"If you don't get out of your own head. Take your ass home, tell that man he shot up the club and the mission was accomplished," she said laughing.

"I thought we were having a girl's day."

"Shut yo' pregnant ass up. I know just like you know time doesn't need to be wasted. It ain't no time like the present to tell that man. I'm sure after you tell him you two will be fucking non-stop. Call me when you come up for air friend."

Since she left the table I took that as my cue to leave as well. Walking to the car I thought about how I could tell Russell that I was pregnant. I know that Russell didn't need all the extra shit. I didn't have the patience for all that anyway so I got in the car and took a deep breath. I started the car and called him after the bluetooth connected to the car.

"What's good baby?" He answered.

"If you could can you meet me at the house or somewhere I need to run something by you?"

"Just bring your fine ass up here to the barbershop. We can talk in the office."

"Okay, I'm about five minutes away because I'm leaving the mall."

"Sounds good to me. I just need to know if I'm gonna need to call a clean-up crew. If I do I can call them now," he said laughing.

"See you in a few minutes Russell."

I ended the call, he has been teasing me since the night I took care of Caretha. It was crazy because he was proud of me like I had graduated at the top of my college class. It was amazing to me that even with all this time apart we were tight like no time had passed at all. The more I thought about it the more I knew that I was indeed tripping thinking that he wasn't going to be happy about the baby. When I arrived at the barbershop it was packed just like it always is. I walked through speaking to everyone but focused on the office door where I knew Russell was waiting on me. I knocked then walked right in. Russell was sitting on the desk smoking a blunt. I closed the door behind me locking it.

"What's going on Adrian?"

"I'm pregnant," I told him.

I don't know why I was so nervous but I was. My hands were sweaty so I was rubbing my palms on my jeans. He studied me for a while as he continued to smoke his blunt.

He let the blunt hang from his mouth as he walked over to me.

"Why you looking so scared about it?"

"I wasn't sure how you were going to react. I know that we just got back in each other's lives. We're about to get married. I just didn't know if being pregnant put too much pressure on you or a strain on our relationship."

He took the blunt out of his mouth holding it in his hand still studying my face. It was as if he was trying to look through me instead of at me. I don't know what he was looking for but, it was making me uncomfortable as fuck.

"You know everything you just named was bullshit right. It doesn't matter how long we haven't been with each other. We're together now that's all that fucking counts. I know you're not cheating on me so there ain't a reason for you to be standing there looking like you're about to pass the fuck out."

"You're happy about the baby?" I asked.

"Fuck yeah I'm happy. I've been trying to knock you up since the first time I felt your walls around my dick. On some real shit I was getting nervous that my shit wasn't working right. I kept getting pissed every month your damn period came. If you weren't pregnant when we came back from the wedding; I was gonna make a doctor's appointment to make sure my dick wasn't broke," he said with a chuckle.

He wrapped his arms around me, kissed me on my forehead. I was so relieved that a couple of tears fell. This man was everything to me. Now he was going to be my husband and the father of my kid. There was a time when I thought the happiness that I was feeling right now would never come to me.

"I love you Russell with everything that I am," I told him.

"Yo, you're only five minutes and two-seconds pregnant and you're already emotional. Oh hell nah, I need a recount. I'm not gonna be dealing with twelve different personalities for the next how ever many months it's gonna take for my princess to get here," he told me while he was still holding me tight.

"You play all day."

"Now you know you're gonna have to lock the gun up now. I can't have the mother of my children knocking bitches off out here in these streets," he said joking.

"You get on my damn nerves. Why do you always say that? That was a one-time thing. I'm not trying to become a hit woman or nothing like that. I just do what I have to do to protect my family."

"Damn Adrian, say that last part again. You sounded sexy as fuck when you said it. As a matter of fact drop them tight ass jeans and bend over on the desk. I want you to say that shit while I'm hitting from the back. That shit's gonna sound sexy as hell watch."

I shook my head but, did as he asked me to. He didn't give me a chance to get comfortable before he was pushing himself inside me. I promise every time we made love I had to give myself a few minutes to adjust to his size. He gave me a few slow strokes before speeding up. He smacked me on the ass before sliding his thumb in my ass.

"Ahhh," I moaned.

"That's not what I want to hear babygirl. Say that sexy shit for me."

"Uh, I do what I gotta do to protect my family," I called out.

"Oh shit yeah, say that shit again baby. Keep saying that shit till I bust up in you. With your fine ass," he grunted.

I did as he asked. It seemed like every time I said it his strokes got faster and harder. I didn't want him to stop pounding me. I could tell by his breathing that he was about to come. I didn't want him to come just like I didn't want him to pull out of me. When he pulled out I always felt empty for the first few minutes. It was like my brain was trying to convince my heart that all of this wasn't a dream.

"Ohhhh Fuck!" He said as he orgasmed. Feeling his orgasm triggered mine.

He pulled out of me going to the bathroom that was in his office. He came back with a warm soapy washcloth. He wiped me off then took it back in the bathroom. The second time he came out with a towel to dry me off. After drying me off he went to clean himself up while I pulled up my pants. Once he was finished he came and gave me a kiss.

"I love you."

"You better I'm your baby daddy woman," he said with the biggest smile.

"No, you're my future husband and my unborn's father. Baby daddy and baby mama sounds so damn ghetto."

He laughed at me and went out of the office door.

"ALL Y'ALL MOTHERFUCKERS CALL ME DADDY BECAUSE A NIGGA'S GOT A BABY ON THE WAY. I SHOT THE CLUB UP AND DIDN'T MISS. NAH, BUT, HOLD UP YOU DOWN LOW NIGGA'S JUST KEEP CALLING ME RUSS. Y'ALL DON'T WANT THESE PROBLEMS. I'M BOUT TO HAVE MY LIL' PRINCESS THOUGH. Y'ALL KEEP YOUR LITTLE HARD HEADS AWAY FROM HER. I DON'T BEAT LIL' KIDS BUT, I'LL SHOOT A LIL' NIGGA FOR TRYING TO PUSH UP ON MY BABY AT THE PLAYGROUND!!"

I laughed at him because he was already doing the most. I wasn't sure how far along I was but, I knew it was too early for him to be talking about his lil' princess. I can't believe I was hesitant about telling him. *Lord help me.*

untie GiGi

"Georgette you are absolutely beautiful tonight."

This man was always complimenting me on how I dressed or wore my hair. There was no way he could be as young as he is. Here I was a forty-nine year old woman being wooed daily by a thirty-seven year old man that proved that love has no age limit. He said as long as two people are above the legal age of consent and mature enough to handle a relationship with a drastic age difference there's nothing that love won't let them accomplish.

"Hector you never talk about your family. You've met mine and you will be seeing them again when you come with me to Vegas for the wedding. I don't even know how many brothers or sisters that you have. Why is that?"

He peered up at me as he took a sip of his water. I could see that he was contemplating what he wanted to say.

"I don't talk about my family because there isn't much to tell. My father came here after making enough money working the cocoa fields to immigrate to the United States. He met my mother three years after getting here. He was working in a bodega in Harlem. She was going to college at NYU at the time. They started hanging out then, here I come. They never got married or had any other children. They stayed together but, didn't care enough to make it official. It wasn't my father's call though. He would've married her twenty-six times if she let him."

"Why didn't she want to get married?"

"I think she was scared of marriage, and love. My grandfather used to beat the shit out of my nana. All of the older woman in my family went through the same thing. So the institute of marriage wasn't a big thing on her side of the family. My father's side was the polar opposite. They believe in being married and fruitful. He put his beliefs aside to make my mother happy. They were loyal to each other but, they just never got married. It was funny because everyone in the neighborhood thought they were married until my father passed. My mother was sure that the obituary was correct by not naming her as his wife but, the owner of his heart. The crazy thing is that I didn't understand that they loved me in ways my friends who had married parents envied. My father taught me to pay attention to what a woman says as well as what she doesn't say."

"Who did you learn all the sexual stuff from?"

"Really, Georgette that's what you want to know," he said laughing at me.

"I've always wondered. You're the first guy that I've experienced that type of dominance with. It's just that you're so good at it."

I had to shift in my seat as I talked to him about the sexual things that we've done. Maybe, I should say that he's done to me because that was the best way to describe it. He had sexual power over me but, he wasn't an asshole about it. There wasn't an ego that I had to constantly appease or tip toe around. He gave me the utmost respect in public. It was in the bedroom or should I say, in sexual situations that he took total control. I loved every minute of it.

"While I was in college I had to find a way to handle my anger and frustrations without putting myself in a set of hand cuffs. I tried boxing, kick boxing, and even rock climbing. All of those activities only made me physically tired. It did nothing for my mental though. I got involved with this chic that loved to be choked during sex. I'm not saying the type of choking I did with you but, she liked to black out and all types of shit. The first time she passed out on me, she came so hard that I thought I broke her. When she came too she wanted to do the shit again. That night she showed me all types of shit that I had never seen before. I started doing my own research when I wasn't studying or fucking her. The more I researched the deeper I got into it. I don't do it with everyone I sleep with though. Not everyone has the strength to be a submissive even if it's just in the bedroom. Most women don't understand that allowing a man to take control is the purest form of power that there is."

"If you're the dominant that means you're in control right? Maybe, I'm missing the point but, being in control equals power doesn't it?" I asked.

"It depends on the people involved. On the surface it may appear that the dominant is in control but, in reality the submissive has the power. I know with me the more I see my submissive enjoying the things that I do to her the more I enjoy it. If you don't enjoy it there's no pleasure in it for me therefore, you have the power," he told me.

"That's a new way of looking at it," I told him.

"If you stick around I can give you a new way of looking at a lot of things."

"Are you into the multiple girlfriends or wives type of thing?"

"No, I hate to share. I was an only child so everything I had was mine and mine alone. I like to keep it that way."

"Is the dominant thing the only unorthodox thing that you're into?" I asked.

"I also love older women," he said licking his lips.

I had to clear my throat because my eyes went directly to his tongue that was licking his medium sized lips. His dark perfectly trimmed goatee had been my seat many of nights. To see his sexy ass mouth and nose coated with my essence was an aphrodisiac for sure. His eyes were light brown with traces of green in them. His hair was dark and curly, eyebrows were a perfect fit for his oval shaped eyes and face. He was built due to him spending a lot of his down time in the gym. I was sitting across from one of those instagram MCM's that random woman would post. The difference was that he was mine, ALL MINE.

"Georgette!" Hector called my name.

"Yes, Hector," I replied causing him to smile showing his perfect set of teeth.

"Is your pussy wet?" He asked.

"Yes."

"Why is your pussy wet? Before you answer understand that I want all the details no matter how insignificant it is to you."

"When you licked your bottom lip with your tongue it caused me to reminisce about all the times I stood over you lowering my pussy to your mouth. Once I was seated comfortably on your mouth you would explore my pussy with your tongue until I orgasmed all over your mouth, chin, and nose. Just the thoughts in my head caused my pussy to get wet," I answered.

He studied me again. I think studying me was one of his favorite things to do. At first it bothered me, it felt like he was trying to read my actions or words. I wasn't concerned about if he thought I was being untruthful with him. I was trying to stop my body's reaction to him. Just being around him caused my nipples to get hard before he said a word or touched me.

"Say it," he told me.

"What is it that you expect for me to say?"

"I want you to say what you were thinking before I told you to say what was on your mind."

"I've been turned out by a young, sexy, doctor that I met at a gas station one random night. He pumped my gas and afterwards I followed him to his place so he could pump my ass," I said with a smile.

"I just figured out a nick name for you. I'm going to call you Vee instead of that ghetto ass GiGi that your family calls you."

"Why Vee?"

"Well that part is simple. The V can stand for various characteristics that you possess. A few examples are Vintage Pussy, vice grip pussy, very addictive pussy, everyday I need that pussy, vivid flashbacks of the pussy, I can keep going if you want."

"No, there's no need for that. I get the picture." I said clearing my throat.

"You were already beautiful, intriguing, and special to me. Even so, seeing you get more comfortable with us being together and tapping into your sexual nature has pushed me until I've fallen in love with you Georgette."

Did he just say….

"You love me Hector?"

"Yes, Georgette, I'm in love with you. I know you think it's because of the sex we have but, the love I have only makes the sex better." He stood up putting the white napkin that was in his lap on the table. I thought he was going to the bathroom so

I went back to eating my food. A weird feeling came over me prompting me to look up. My heart damn near jumped out of my chest seeing Hector down on one knee with a Burgundy velvet box in his hand. I started looking around only to find out the entire restaurant was watching us.

"I know this may seem quick to you but, we don't have any time to waste. I want to wake up to you, come home to you, have you bring me lunch sometimes, I'll even go play bingo and Zumba with you. I don't care how much older you are than me. The only thing that matters to me is if you will allow me to show you a different side of life for the rest of your life. Say yes to being my wife?" Hector said.

"YES! Hector, oh shit, hell yes!" I told him.

The entire restaurant was clapping, whistling, and tapping their glasses with their silverware. *I can't believe I'm finally getting married.*

CHAPTER 20

race

Today was the last fitting before the wedding. A normal bride would have the men and the ladies doing separate fittings, not Adrian and Russell. Everyone was getting fitted except for Adrian. She was here in full bridezilla fashion though. It was funny to see Adrian so nervous and extra when Russell was just chilling. Adrian didn't have any family around her so Uncle Geoff was going to give her away. Gully was the best man while Rick, Uncle Geon, Uncle Gary, Hector, and Russell's friend Quell were the groomsmen. I was the maid of honor with Quell's girlfriend, Auntie GiGi, my assistant Alexia, Uncle Gary's woman and, Uncle Geon's current whatever she was to him. I looked around and realized quick as hell that this is going to be the most ghetto wedding Las Vegas was ever going to see.

I was glad to see Uncle Geoff finally up and walking around. Those hearts attacks he had a few months ago scared me to death. I'm not ready to bury any of my family just yet. Uncle Geoff was doing really good. I asked him what motivated him to go so hard in therapy he told me that 'eating that nasty ass prison food was my motivation'. He swore that the prisons and the hospitals used the same company for cooks.

"I need to let y'all know that Hector proposed to me last night and I said yes," Auntie GiGi said holding her hand up for everyone to see.

"I'm calling the medical board on his ass in the morning. If he proposed to your stale ass he has to be taking more drugs than he's prescribing. It has to be drugs or he has mommy issues," Uncle Geoff joked.

"Ha, ha hell. You better not get too happy with those jokes over there you weak hearted mother fucker. Why can't your ass be a normal brother and be happy for your baby sister?" Auntie GiGi asked.

"Your ass ain't a damn baby no more GiGi. You're just younger now, you're the YOUNGER sister because, there ain't nothing baby-like about your ancient ass."

"If I'm ancient that make you prehistoric then doesn't it. Just make sure you're at my wedding when the time comes."

"What if I'm busy that day?" Uncle Geoff asked.

I don't know why they always loved getting on Auntie GiGi's nerves.

"Just be ready to die the next day. If you don't come to my wedding I'm gonna come for you," she told him.

"Congratulations sis," Uncle Geon said making everyone stop and look at him. He usually was going back and forth with Auntie GiGi too. For him not to try her was strange.

"Nigga if you ain't got the pussy yet you're not gonna get it. I know you're not trying to show off because that bitch is here with you. I'm saying she's coming to Las Vegas with you free of charge she ain't gonna say nothing against you until we get back from Vegas. You can be your true self brother. You know we don't put on for these hoes," Uncle Geoff said.

"That's some cold shit to say man. You need to stop tripping on GiGi like that. Can't we all just get along?" Uncle Gary asked.

Everyone was laughing at them go back and forth. Even the two ladies that were helping us were laughing. My family is so embarrassing. I didn't choose them but, Adrian did and she loved us all to death. I couldn't understand why she didn't pick a family that wasn't blessed with so many mental patients.

"Nah Gary don't try to get his evil ass straight. It don't have anything to do with Treasure being here. GiGi needs a man to get her mind right, so what's the problem?" Uncle Geon asked.

"I know y'all are her brothers and all that but, you're not gonna keep talking about her like that," Hector said.

"Oh shit y'all did you hear that? We've pissed off a Cuban he's gonna leave here and call El Chapo to kill our asses. Keep your head on a swivel bro. When you go to the car make sure you run in a zig zag line so the snipers can't get a clean shot," Uncle Geoff said making everyone laugh harder.

I don't know where they came up with this shit.

"El Chapo was Mexican Pop," Rick said.

"Mexican, Cuban what's the difference they're all kingpins and shit. I'll put it like this then. We can't be pissing him off or the Cartels are gonna come cut our tongues out for talking slick," Uncle Geoff said.

"Why do you keep saying we? You're the only one fucking with the man. Aye Hector, check this out. If you call somebody on him make sure they're aiming at his ass and not me. You're good for Georgette's mean ass the way I see it. His big head ass is just mad because he sees her happy finally," Uncle Gary said.

"How you gonna throw me under the bus like that?" Uncle Geoff asked.

"I ain't throw you under a damn thing. You crawled under that motherfucker on your own by standing here fucking with the man. I ain't trying to die over your bullshit," Uncle Gary said.

"If I call the Cartels then I supposed I should be looking for the color coordinated gang bangers to come looking for me then huh? Since I'm the one fucking the shit out of your sister in the most disrespectful way every night," Hector said.

"Oh shit!" Russell and Gully said at the same time.

"Now see I was just on some ha-ha bullshit with your andale-andale ass. You telling me about you sexing my sister is just disrespectful," Uncle Geoff said.

"Would you rather I just forward you one of the videos instead?" Hector asked.

Uncle Geoff looked like he wanted to throw up. Uncle Gary was laughing and shaking his head. Uncle Geon looked confused and Auntie GiGi was smiling hard as hell.

"She put it on you that bad man that you gotta put her business out there like that?" Uncle Geon said.

"You motherfuckers gonna stop coming for my man and our relationship like that. Don't worry about how good I put it on him. I respect y'all relationships with all the scalawags. Yes, we're getting married and I dare one of y'all to say one more slick comment and I'm beating all y'all asses. After I'm finish Hector can fix y'all up. Are we here to try on our gear or to listen to frick and frat talk about me?"

"I hope y'all don't act up like this during the weekend. I can't handle y'all acting up. The people in Vegas don't know that y'all aren't serious," Adrian said.

"I can see it now. We're gonna have to go down the police station to bond you and whoever you were fighting out."

"Grace, it's hard to believe that they raised you," Germain said trying to be funny.

"You got jokes but, you're volunteering to be in this family. They did a damn good job of raising me too. If you think they didn't then you tell them, not me."

"Nah, I'm good on that."

We went back to watching them insult each other. Quell and his girlfriend had ducked off somewhere to be nasty. Auntie GiGi and Hector were all into each other just like everyone else was. Afterwards, we all went to eat a local soul food restaurant. Scanning the room I realize that we were all representing the *Black Love* that so many people on social media searched for. This was the most beautiful thing that I've seen all year. You don't see many images like the one I was a part of these days.

"Cuz, how are you doing? I know I've been a little busy lately. We don't talk like we used to. What's going on with you? I see that you and Gully are back kicking it. I'm proud of you for changing for him," Rick said.

"Change? What are you talking about? I didn't change," I told him.

"You did change but, it's a good change so it's all good," he nonchalantly added.

"I haven't changed Rick."

"Yes you have. Think about it from the outside looking in. You're smiling more, you haven't been a bitch, and he's changed too."

"Give me more precise examples."

"That's easy, for starters we've been here for a good little while and you having called one person here an asshole. That's big considering you come from a long line of assholes. The staff at the lounge has been saying that you're easier to talk to and that you're less demanding."

"You've been talking about me to my employees?" I asked.

"No, I was there the other night minding my black ass business when the bartender asked if I was your cousin. When I told her I was she asked had you hit the lottery or something lately. When I asked her why that's what she told me. I may have spoken too soon because you're about to get all defensive on me now. You don't have to be all like that about it. Take the compliment, say thank you, then life goes on."

"How can you see that as a compliment?" I asked.

"That's what it is. We don't want the old Grace back. We like this version of you. Everyone likes this version of you. It's safer for all of us. I know the relationship thing is new for you but, embrace that shit. Happiness looks good on both of y'all."

"Thank you Rick. When are you going to settle down? You're eligible and handsome and you have a little bit of money. There's no reason for you to be single."

"I hope what you just said goes from your mouth to god's ears. I'm not ready for all that yet. I love being home alone at night. I don't have a nagging ass female bothering me about shit that doesn't have anything to do with her."

"I hear you. I still say there's a perfect woman out there for you. Everyone has their own person that was made for them. I want you to experience love without question or doubt," I told him.

He looked at me and started laughing.

"Yeah he's done fucked all the bitch up out of you," he said laughing.

"Kiss my ass Rick," I told him.

Seeing everyone together made me miss my dad. Only if he

could be here right now everyone that I hold near and dear to my heart would be here. I felt a little bit of sadness because of him not being her but, I was happy to be able to feel the love that was in this room.

CHAPTER 21

ully

The weekend of the wedding is finally here. I was expecting to close on our new house the same week we get back. This was a well needed vacation for Grace and I. We were doing good since we've gotten back together. She was excited about the wedding which I fully expected. I couldn't tell if she was just happy for Adrian or if she's using this wedding to drum up ideas for ours. We haven't discussed marriage yet but, none of that mattered to me.

"We're here," Russell said.

I could see that Russell was trying to play it cool right now. He had been sick off and on since he found out about Adrian being pregnant. He looked like he was going to pass out while Adrian was chilling doing the crossword puzzle she started before we boarded the plane.

"Are you good over there Russ? You're looking a little pale over there," I said to him.

"Man I've been sick as fuck for the past two days. I can't seem to get it together. I have to lay down when we get to the room. Hopefully, I can sleep off whatever it is that I have going on," he told me.

"You can't fix what's going on with you. You're having sympathy symptoms of the pregnancy. You're getting her weak stomach, constant nausea, cold sweats, and being emotional as hell for nothing."

I shook my head at Auntie GiGi's words. I knew she had just hit it right on the head what was wrong with Russ.

"That's nice to know. I gotta deal with this shit until she has the baby?"

"It depends on you. Some men only have it for a short time others have been known to have it for the entire pregnancy."

"I know we're supposed to hang out with y'all tonight but, I think Adrian and I are gonna crash in the room for the night. We'll check with y'all in the morning for breakfast."

Everyone checked into their rooms and agreed to meet back up in an hour to spend our first night on the town. Tomorrow is Friday and that's the start of the wedding weekend festivities. I had the entire itinerary memorized. Adrian had texted it to everyone in addition talking about it for most of the flight here. She also handed everyone a paper copy of the itinerary. Adrian was doing the most but, everyone was letting her have her weekend.

"Are you ready to kill the town with me baby?" I asked Grace as we walked to the elevator.

"Oh yeah, you have to remember what happens in Vegas stays in Vegas," she said laughing.

"Nah, that's that reckless thot shit. We're making memories this weekend. I'm talking about some shit that we can tell our kids and grandkids."

"You're tripping, how can it be reckless thot shit if everyone here is coupled up? I will be a thot for my man anytime," she said giving me a kiss.

The slow ass elevator finally came. For the Stratosphere Casino and hotel to be a high profile place the elevators sucked. When it got to us there was a bunch of people waiting to get on with us so I couldn't get freaky with her and I waited for us to get to the room. When we got to the room Grace's first move was to the bathroom. She was in there taking selfies like she was an instagram model. I laid across the bed thinking I was going to get a couple of minutes of a nap before we hung out tonight.

"How long are you gonna be in the bathroom? I want to squeeze on your ass cheeks while I take my nap," I said.

"I know you're not sleeping. We're in Vegas Germain. You're not up and ready to get to the streets. We don't have to leave the hotel there's plenty to do here. We could even go get on one of the rollercoasters. This is my first time in Vegas so get up. They can call us on one of our cell phones when they're ready to meet up. Adrian and Russ aren't coming out so it's just us and the other people," she told me.

"Those other people are your family. I'm telling Auntie GiGi you don't want to hang with her and El Chapo's homeboy," I said laughing.

"I can't believe the things that come out of their mouths sometimes. When he said that Hector was gonna call El Chapo I almost died in that bridal shop," she said laughing.

She was right we never knew what they were going to say but, that made them authentic. They talked a lot of shit to each other but, when they needed each other they were there no questions asked. I had to shut them down because they wanted to take Grace to one of their houses but, she belonged home with me. I was gonna take care of her fuck everyone else. I had her for the rest of her life, they understood that shit now.

"Yeah, that shit was wild. I was fucking impressed that Hector spoke up. They were just testing his ass. I don't know why though because, if Hector can deal with Auntie GiGi and her mouth we know damn well he can handle your Uncles."

"You've got a point there," Grace told me.

I sat up on the bed since it was obvious that Grace wasn't going to let me rest. I figured that she would've been to Vegas before now. It wasn't like she didn't have the means to get out and see the world.

"Why you've never been here before?"

"I was too busy trying to make my dreams come true. It takes hard work to open a cigar lounge in a part of town that has liquor stores and bodegas on the corners. The fact that I was a woman only made it harder. To the old white men downtown being a woman is worse than being black. A vacation was on my, to do list. I never thought about coming to Vegas though. I was thinking somewhere more tropical."

"You must've been scared to let loose. Grace promise me you'll let ya hair down this weekend. Just go with the flow," I said to her.

"I'll try to let loose."

Hearing her say that she was going to try was good enough for me. I was going to get my woman tore up tonight. I just hope that we wake up not too hung over tomorrow.

OOOO

Vegas was about to be on my yearly vacation destination list. Grace was acting like a kid in a candy store with all the lights and sounds surrounding us. She managed to convince my ass to go on this bullshit ass ride that was at the Stratosphere where we were staying. I admit that I had fun once I got on the damn thing. It was a regular rollercoaster car ride. It rode you away from the hotel in the air for a good distance then, it stops. It makes you think that you're just hanging in the air. You hang there for a little bit then it reverses you fast as hell. That ride was better than the one that you sit in the big merry-go-round thing and it lets you hang over the Vegas strip. I was looking at everyone get on and off of it but, I wasn't getting up there. It would be the one time I get up there for it to malfunction while I'm dangling in the air.

After the rides we walked up and down the street. There was a bar and strip joint everywhere you looked. There were street vendors that were trying to sell everything from pussy to star maps. On one corner we passed a preaching man dressed like Elvis Presley a block away there was another one dressed as Michael Jackson.

When we were done walking the strip and drinking drinks from every spot that sold alcohol. We ended up in Fat Tuesday's which was located at the hotel and casino that we were staying in. I didn't want to see the sights and all that. I just wanted Grace to enjoy her first time here. She was singing, dancing, and talking to people as they walked by. This was a side of her that I hadn't seen yet. Coming here wasn't only a vacation for me but, I came to see that Grace needed this more than I did. Seeing her laugh and joke was more memorable to me. I know she's not going to remember half of the shit she's done but, that was the fun of it all. I even got out there on the floor with her a few times. I didn't have to worry about any of the guys pushing up on her because she was singing and dancing around tell everyone that 'fine ass Gully was her man'. The shit was comical as hell. It made it more amusing that I knew she wasn't gonna remember shit in the morning. I also knew she was going be hung over something terrible.

CHAPTER 22

 race

Last night was so much fun that I hardly remember any of it. Germain woke me up this afternoon around one or two to make sure I ate then I went back to sleep. It's now five in the evening and I'm finally waking up on my own. I had a slight headache and my mouth tasted like nothing but, cotton.

"You're up," Germain said as I walked in to the living room area of our room.

"How long have you been up?"

"I never went back to sleep after we ate breakfast. I went down to the gym to workout, got back here took a shower and I've been looking at TV ever since. How do you feel?"

"I feel like I'll never take your advice and let loose again. I don't even remember all of last night. I know we were playing blackjack then I got on the slot machines. After that I don't know what happen," I told him.

I don't know what he thought but, I wasn't going to be drinking like I did last night. It was crazy that even in college I'd gone to parties here and there but, I never got as drunk as I did last night. I was glad that I was surrounded with family though because I was a prime candidate for sex trafficking. I know I can say that I wasn't going to drink tonight but, with the things that we have planned for the guys I was definitely going to have to get drunk. I don't know how Adrian was going to make it with all those people looking at us. She didn't have the club shut down so there were going to be a ton of strangers looking as we did what was planned. Yup, I was definitely going to be drunk again tonight.

OOOOOO

This place was packed. I know that people were always talking about the Vegas night life but, the way the people were shoulder to shoulder in here was ridiculous. If all the clubs were like this every night then the owners were making a killing in here. Adrian had thought about the crowd ahead of time by reserving two VIP sections for us. Everyone was having a great time. Auntie GiGi and her brother's aren't acting up in here everyone was smiling and enjoying life. This was a great moment in life. It was about to be epic because it was showtime.

"Okay ladies we have a bathroom run to make," Adrian said standing to her feet.

"Let me find out y'all are on some freaky leaky shit. Why do chic's always go to the bathroom together? They use the bathroom at home alone," Quell slurred.

He usually didn't do much talking when we were all around each other. The liquor had him talking as much shit as my family member s tonight though. Instead of going back and forth with him us ladies got up and headed to the bathroom. In reality we were going to a dressing room in the club. Adrian and I had everything set up for our little performance for the guys tonight. I was nervous as hell due to the fact that I've never done anything like this before and to do it in front of a packed club of strangers was a bit much for me. We were all in the room getting dressed. I'm sure everyone else was as nervous as I was. The entire bridal party was in here quiet as hell just changing clothes. There was a knock on the door.

"You ladies have about ten minutes, take your shots now," one of the security guys said.

"Let's go make our men realize why they chose us to be their women," Quell's girlfriend said.

I took two shots of some white liquor. I didn't know what the name of it was but, once the burn started in my chest I realized that it had to be tequila. I had already taken two so why not another. After downing the last shot I followed the other ladies out onto the dance floor.

The dance floor was cleared except for the chairs that the guys sat in. The chairs were in a triangular formation with Russ at the front. We stood off to the side so they couldn't see us. We were dressed in a pair of fishnet stockings, with a uniform that was similar to the uniforms that *The Radio City Rockettes* wear it was a one piece that looked like a butler's uniform. The black top hats, black stiletto's and the black cane completed the look. The lights shut off followed by spotlights on each guy. The beat dropped letting us know it was show time. We walked out slowly as Beyonce's song Flaws and All played through the speakers. We walked in true top model fashion. We were all in full stripper mode as we circled the men stopping in front of them. Our right legs were up and over their shoulders. We started rubbing the cane on their chests. We could hear the clapping and yelling from the crowd. Taking our hats off we put them on the guys heads. Removing our legs from their shoulders we turned and touched our ankles.

Our asses were directly in their faces. Germain smacked and kissed my ass which I should've known was coming. We started moving our hips in circular motions as we dropped slowly to the floor. Turning we were now on our knees in front of them.

"I'm gonna fuck the shit out of you when we get to the room," Gully told me making me laugh.

We put our heads in their laps and started moving them around to make it appear that we were giving them fellatio. After staying down there for a few minutes we eased our way up to stand between their legs. Next, we straddled their laps, beginning to rise up and down while facing them to give the appearance of riding their dicks. Gully's hands went to my ass. I'm sure the rest of the ladies were getting groped right now as well. When the song went off we were still on their laps slightly turned so that we were looking at the crowd. I saw that Adrian and Russ were damn near fucking though.

"What did you think?" I asked Gully once I got back on my feet.

He looked at me licked his lips and gripped his hard dick through his pants. I got the message loud and clear.

"Oh you're not gonna be able to get down the aisle Sunday morning. I'm tearing your ass up as soon as we get back to the room."

"Let me go change back into my clothes and I'll be back out."

I left before he could stop me. I knew that they were going to like the performance but, Gully was acting like he wanted to fuck me right then and there.

"Oh my goodness y'all that was so bomb,"Adrian said excitedly.

"I don't know about y'all but, I might get pregnant tonight. I thought Hector was gonna try to get the goods right there on the dance floor in front of all those people. It's a good thing that I bought my uniform because that baby is going home with me," Auntie GiGi said.

When we got back to our section Gully handed me a filled shot glass. I threw it back and the second one he gave me after that. The party was in full swing now. I was standing at the edge of the balcony of the VIP section looking at all the people party. I felt Gully come behind me grinding his dick into my ass.

"Adrian and Russ just left. You know since they're both pregnant they turned in early. I doubt if we see them until Sunday before the wedding. I can't wait to make you my wife," he whispered in my ear.

"Why wait?" I heard myself asking.

"Stop fucking with me Grace."

"I'm not. It's not like we weren't planning to do it anyway. You're always talking about how we don't have any more time to waste. So let's do it."

"Are you serious?" He asked as he moved to stand beside me.

"Yeah, but, damn that's gonna take away from Adrian's weekend. Let me hit her up first. I'm not trying to cause no problems with her emotional ass."

I took my phone out and texted her.

Me: Best friend I think Germain and I are about to elope

Best Bitch: You would do it after I leave. I actually bet Russell that y'all were gonna do it last night. Go for it get the largest package. I want a ton of pictures

Me: So you're not gonna be pissed if we do it

Best Bitch: go get married with your drunk ass

"What did she say?"

"She said she bet Russ that we were gonna do it last night," I told him laughing.

"Well, that means we're late then."

He took my hand and led me out of the VIP section.

"Where are y'all headed to?" Auntie GiGi asked with Hector kissing all on her neck.

They were so cute together. Even with the age difference it was plain to see that they were in love with each other. Hector was protective of his woman that was for sure. Auntie GiGi didn't play about him either. I was grateful that she's found her soul mate. She had been there for all of us all of our lives. It was good that she had someone to be there for her besides family.

"We're going to elope," I told her with a smile.

Hector looked up.

"Word?" He asked.

"Yeah man, we're in Vegas so why not,"Gully said.

"Well shit, we're coming too."

"Huh, coming where?" Auntie GiGi asked.

"We're going with them to get married Georgette."

"To watch them get married?" She asked.

"No, to get married right beside them now bring ya fine ass on Vee," he said.

"Who the hell is Vee?" I asked.

"Mind your business little girl," Auntie GiGi said with a giggle.

We left the club and headed for the first chapel. *I's getting married*.

CHAPTER 23

drian

Tonight is the night that I'm going it marry the only man I've ever loved. All my family was here and that's all I could ever ask for. I was so nervous that I couldn't stop crying. They weren't tears of fear or regret though. These were happy tears so I just let them flow. It was so bad that I told the make-up artist just give me some lip gloss, eye shadow, and make sure my eyebrows were right. If I put on mascara or foundation it was going to end up running down my face by the time the wedding was over. I still paid her but, there was no need to be that extra just to end up looking a mess by the time pictures were to be taken.

"Are you nervous enough?" Grace asked me.

"Yup I've been crying since he left the room earlier today. Thank you so much for being here for me all these years. You are so much more than a best friend to me. How does it feel to be somebody's wife?" I asked her.

"Oh you'll find out in a little bit. I see why you picked this place. Everything is so beautiful, it's so classy in here that it makes me feel kind of ratchet for not having any panties on," she laughed.

"I know we're close but, that was too much information. I'm telling you now if you and Gully are in some room fucking when it's time for the wedding party to be introduced; I'm going to get on the mic and tell everybody what you're up to," I said laughing.

"Everybody like who? You need to be worried about your Auntie and her fountain of youth doing all that. I'm not even gonna speak on her brothers. They are my uncles but, they are prime candidates to be fucking in the janitor's closet," she said laughing.

Before I could say anything the rest of the bridal party came in. They were all so beautiful in their blue gowns. We were gonna take some bomb ass pictures with the lights of the strip in the background.

"You're not dressed yet? What's the matter? Does the dress fit?" Auntie GiGi asked.

"I'm waiting for the tears to slow up. I don't want to get my dress wet. It fits even with this little bit of extra weight that I'm carrying around. Can y'all help me put this thing on?" I asked.

"Sure come on," Auntie GiGi said.

"Oh yeah congrats on getting married Auntie GiGi," I told her.

"Thank you Adrian."

"Married? So are we the only ones that are going back home without husbands?" Uncle Geoff's girlfriend said while looking at the other ladies of the wedding party.

"I ain't trying to get married and Gary knows it. Marriage ain't for everybody, so speak for yourself," Uncle Gary's girlfriend said.

"Unless you went and got married last-night then yeah. Y'all are the ones that are leaving Vegas with the same status you got here with. I know you didn't think that you were going to get married on this trip. I don't know about Quell but, I know my brothers or nephew ain't marrying a damn thing. If you gonna sit here and start some shit about it just wait until the pictures get done so I can punch you right in your shit when you start it up," Auntie GiGi said.

"Oh Lordy, Auntie don't start please," Grace said.

"Don't Auntie me. She knows damn well those niggas ain't trying to get married. If she wanted to be part of the family she was better off telling him that she was his long lost daughter. He'll claim anybody's child but, he damn sure ain't marrying anybody's daughter."

"Stop talking bout your brother's children," I said.

Auntie GiGi went in her purse pulling out some paperwork.

"Read this with your own eyes. Those hoe's and that big back gorilla ain't shit to me. You can claim them if you want to but, I ain't claiming shit without a proper DNA test. Y'all thought I was just talking shit to be talking but, I was dead ass serious," Auntie Gigi said.

Grace and I looked at the paperwork and sure enough it said that they were not their children.

"How did you get this?" Grace asked the million dollar question.

"I went to the damn store and bought a DNA test for each of them. While they were up at the hospital acting all family-like I got their samples. All I had to do was go to Gary and Geon's house to get some hair from their brushes. I put it together and sent the shit off. I'm giving it to them tonight after the wedding," she said.

"That's messy," I said.

"Well, just call me Messy Ass Mae then. I needed answers fuck all that," she said.

"That ain't gonna do nothing but, start an argument," I said.

"Oh well another day another truth told," she responded.

Auntie GiGi knows she needs to stop her stuff. I just hope and pray that they don't start fighting in here tonight.

"Pray for her," I told Grace.

"The family grew like a motherfucker this weekend didn't it," Auntie GiGi said dancing around the room.

While we were all laughing at her there was a knock on the door.

"It's show time," a lady said from the other side of the door.

"Come hop your ass in this dress. I plan to be riding my husband's dick as the sun comes up in the morning," Auntie GiGi said.

"Too much information," Grace said with her face balled up.

GiGi and Grace helped me into my dress while the other ladies tried to get the stuff that I brought with me together to go back to our hotel room. The hotel had someone to take the stuff back while the ceremony was going on. Once the dress was on the three of us took a selfie for me to post later on tonight or in the morning. The lady came back and walked us to the doorway were everyone would be walking down the aisle that led to the balcony that we were getting married on with the live Vegas strip in the back ground. I stood there shaking as they all went down the aisle one my one. Just before it was time for me to go the lady passed me a note saying that she was told to give it to me. I unfolded it.

Adrian,
Wipe your face and bring your ass down here to marry me. If I cry don't

tell nobody back home. Nah, on second thought you can tell whoever you
want that I cried. I'm not crying because of what we've gone through.
I'm crying because whatever the future holds for us I know that we'll get
through it together. If I bust my gun I know you'll be right there busting
yours beside me. Don't get too worked up and have my baby coming out
with a nervous tick. I love you and hurry the hell up,
Yo Damn Husband Russell

I looked up and the lady opened the doors. There he was crying looking at me. I was crying looking at him. I had to laugh at the fact that both of us were all to pieces. I took a deep breath and took my first step to meet my husband at the altar in my white dress.

OOOO

The reception was live as hell for it just to be us in there. We were having a ball. From what I could see no-one has gone to find a janitor's closet to get nasty in yet.

"Is this thing on?"Auntie GiGi asked tapping on the microphone that she held in her hand.

"Oh shit," I said as I looked for Grace.

Grace was standing behind Gully trying to hide her face. Gully and Russell were looking confused.

"It's on we hear you," Gully called out only to be hit in the back by Grace.

"I have something that I want to say. Congratulations to Russell and Adrian first before I get to the meat and potatoes of why I'm up here. Y'all are a beautiful couple. I wish y'all nothing but happiness and a bunch of babies. I have something to say to my brothers. I love y'all with all my heart but, I'm not going to continue this charade with y'all any longer."

"What the hell is you talking about Georgette?" Uncle Geon said.

"I just want y'all to know that when we get back home you both need to go see a lawyer to take those heathens off your wills and stuff. I'm not talking about you Geoff. This is for Geon and Gary."

"Heathens?" Uncle Gary asked.

"Yup those kids that I told y'all when they were born that they weren't y'all's. I'm talking about those heathens. I have the proof right here. This paperwork proves that we don't have any forty-dollar whores or gorillas in the mist in our family. Y'all can take these copies because I have the originals."

She put the mic down and handed them both the papers in her hand. Gully and Russell were laughing their selves to tears. Hector was shaking his head but, he didn't say anything to her.

"Ain't this some shit," Uncle Gary said as he pulled his phone out and started dialing numbers. Uncle Geon was right behind him with his phone stuck to his face.

"Auntie GiGi knows she wrong as hell for that shit," Russell said laughing still.

The rest of us danced the night away.

"How does it feel to be a wife?" Grace asked me.

"Oh it's lit being a wife," I responded as we hugged.

EPILOGUE

It was crazy how one night led to so much drama and finally happiness. Auntie GiGi and Hector ended up adopting some pre-teen twin boys that they were raising as their own now. They decided to adopt because it would be easier on them. Auntie GiGi didn't want a baby or a younger child because she didn't have time for pampers and car seats. My uncles are still the playa-playa's that they always were. When they found out that the kids that they took care of all of their lives weren't theirs they were pissed at Auntie GiGi for a while but, they got over it. She was only trying to help. She told them that if they would've listened to her when she said it all those years ago they wouldn't have to go through all this mess now. The kids in question still came around the family but, Auntie GiGi makes them call her Mrs. GiGi instead of Auntie. That lady is a mess. Hector has her ass together though. She knows how far to go.

Adrian and Russ were going hard still. She had a little boy that we call RJ and now she's pregnant with a set of twin girls. This pregnancy is harder on Russ than the first one. He has all the sickness and cravings that the woman usually deals with. He's the one telling everybody that they aren't having any more children after the twins are born. Adrian is loving it because all she has to deal with is the fatigue and some swelling. She's out here living her life big belly and all.

As for Germain and I we are out here opening businesses and making bank. In addition to the lounge and the land acquisition company, we have a daycare, and two more cigar lounges. We haven't gotten pregnant yet but, we try all the time. It'll happen when the time is right. For the time being we are just enjoying our time together and practicing every chance we get.

It's wild how life turns out completely different from the way you planned it in your head. At one point in time I was fine being a single female business owner. Now with the life I have I cringe at the thought of that being all that my life was made up of. If I would've known that just by meeting this man that caught my eye the night of my grand opening that everything I thought was normal would be anything but that. The road we had to take was bumpy but, I wouldn't change the path. That road allowed me to take a long hard look at myself and make some changes. Without doing that I wouldn't be as comfortable as I am to be a boss bitch that knows when to let her man take the lead. That's the type of relationship that Germain and I now have. He knows when to step in and I know that when he steps in it's time for me to step aside. There's nothing wrong or demeaning about it. It's all about respect with us and that's the way it will always be when you look up and see Gully & Grace.

THE END